A SWEET DECEIT

Other books by Lois Schwartz:

When Roses Bloom

A SWEET DECEIT

•

Lois Schwartz

AVALON BOOKS
NEW YORK

111306

F
Sch

Published by Thomas Bouregy & Co., Inc.
160 Madison Avenue, New York, NY 10016

Library of Congress Cataloging-in-Pubication Data

Schwartz, Lois, 1939–
    A sweet deceit / Lois Schwartz.
        p. cm.
    ISBN 0-8034-9805-5 (acid-free paper)
    I. Title.

PS3619.C4874S94 2006
813'.6—dc22

                                        2006018080

PRINTED IN THE UNITED STATES OF AMERICA
ON ACID-FREE PAPER
BY HADDON CRAFTSMEN, BLOOMSBURG, PENNSYLVANIA

To my readers, whose enjoyment of my
books keeps me writing.

Prologue

So far, so good. No one had spotted her.

Ali deGroot pulled into the last parking slot beside the kitchens at the back of the expansive country club. Carefully looking in every direction, she didn't see that anyone had noticed her arrival. She heard doors slam farther down the row of cars. Ali's heart raced as she watched a man and a woman climb out and walk away from her, toward the main entrance, with two children in tow.

She waited until they disappeared from view, then opened her car door and backed out, leaning over to keep her head inside. Carefully putting her keys into a secure hidden pocket inside her vest, she pulled off her shoes and stepped into the large pink fuzzy feet she took from between the front seats. When those were tied on securely, she pulled the white furry legs down over the tops. Then, reaching to the passenger seat, she lifted the giant white head onto the driver's seat. She checked that the long ears faced forward and lifted it up.

Forced to back away from the car for more room, Ali pulled on the head and fastened the Velcro tabs under her chin. Lifting the pink taffeta vest over the flair and straightening the huge bow tie in front to hide the joint, she backed up even farther, her head still out of sight of any late arrivals.

She couldn't see anything that wasn't straight ahead of her. Her only line of vision was through the dark mesh of the eyes and a small area around the two large front teeth. Even so, she had to work fast before she was discovered.

Pulling on the white glove attached to the base of her furry left sleeve, Ali stuck her hand inside and pressed the wrist to secure the hidden closure. After settling her right hand in the other mitt, she pressed the closure against her thigh.

Feet . . . head . . . ears . . . vest . . . mitts. She patted her vest to be certain that her keys were safely stashed and took a deep breath to calm the excitement rippling through her. She already felt warm on the cool spring day. Wearing fur from head to toe would only make her hotter as the afternoon progressed, but it was worth it. She loved pretending to be someone else.

Ali maneuvered her foot-long ears through the front

car door and promptly shut it. One quick reach into the backseat netted her a huge basket with a sturdy handle, filled with dozens of individually wrapped pink eggs.

Another deep breath as she locked the car and she was ready.

Showtime.

She had just walked to the sidewalk leading to the entrance when she was spotted.

"Mommy, look!" a child cried. "He's here already."

Skipping quickly but without spilling her eggs, Ali waved to the child as she rounded the corner of the club building. Without stopping, she passed the entrance and crossed to the manicured grass that sloped gently to the golf cart path. Excited and expectant children and their parents filled the lawn before her.

Happy screams erupted the second they saw her.

"The Easter Bunny is here!" they cried as they ran to surround her.

Her big grin hidden by the rabbit head, Ali slowly walked down the slope, handing out pink eggs and hugs to the children on all sides as she went.

Chapter One

"At least I didn't have to find a teenager to dress up as a chicken for this promotion. Remember the kid last summer who ended up tying sacks of ice around his waist to keep himself cool in the heavy suit?" Ali asked her sister, Helen McBride.

"Isn't he the one who singed his tail feathers by getting too close to the barbecued chickens they were selling?" Helen responded with a laugh.

"Yeah. Caused a little too much excitement for my taste. Thankfully the rest of the costume was fireproof. He spent the rest of the afternoon away from the barbeque area, with only a burned tail to show for the encounter."

"That can't have smelled good."

"The smoky barbeque took care of it. Compared to

that experience, this promotion was effortless, and it was successful too. All the actress I hired had to do was stand in front of the candy store in the mall and pass out a bunch of little bags of old-fashioned candy."

"Hey, if it's the really old-fashioned kind, save me some of those colorful sugar dots on the long strips of white paper. I love those things."

"You have weird taste in food, sis," Ali replied. "I'll save you some strips, but when are you coming for a visit so you can eat them? You haven't even seen my new house, and I moved in just over two months ago."

"What's your neighborhood like?"

"Well, so far I like it. It's quiet, and I love having a backyard where I can relax and think about more than my next promotion job."

"Sounds great, but here I am the married sister and you end up owning a house before I do."

"Well, actually, the bank owns it," Ali replied with a laugh. "But your time will come. Right now a house would be a lot to take care of, with your husband gone so much of the time."

"I suppose. So, you like the house, and your promotions company is always busy, from what you tell me. I'm so happy for you."

"Thanks, sis. Now if I could just have some quiet so I can finish my work at a reasonable hour and get sleep at night."

"I thought you said the neighborhood was quiet."

"It is, except for the new neighbor who moved in

next door about three weeks ago. He comes and goes at very odd hours. The women who pick him up at night pull into the driveway and beep their horns. But maybe I should be thankful he doesn't have kids who play loud music all the time."

"When you get to know his wife, maybe she could get the beeping stopped."

"He doesn't have a wife—not one that I've seen, anyway. The same woman picks him up most of the time, but there are other women too."

"Oh, really?" Helen said hopefully. "What's the man like?"

"As a matter of fact, he's tall, good-looking, and probably not more than a few years older than I am—thirty-five at the outside."

"Oh, really?" Helen asked, raising her voice in more hopeful speculation. "And you're sure he's not married?"

Ali laughed. "Uh-oh, I'm sorry I mentioned him. Quit your matchmaking, Helen. I'm not ready to get involved with another man at this point. I don't bounce back very well after I've been lied to and stolen from by my fiancé when I thought I was on the way to being married."

"Sounds awful when you put everything Jeff did in a list like that. I know you're still hurting, hon. But you shouldn't let him hurt you more by making you miserable for such a long time. He took off with your money two years ago."

"Thank goodness I found out about him before we

were married." Ali sighed. "But enough about him. When can you come see my neat new house?"

"I'll let you know as soon as I can," Helen promised. "I'll try to set it up for the next time Eric is gone, which, knowing his schedule, won't be a long wait," she added unhappily.

"Just let me know when to expect you, and I'll be at the Syracuse airport with bells on."

"Thanks for giving me a ride home," Jase VanDam told his office assistant, Roxanne Warner.

"I don't mind, especially when you buy the gas. Besides, bringing you to your new house is faster than driving all the way to that condo you had. But, um . . . my husband is beginning to wonder when your car will be ready."

Jase laughed. "Is he getting jealous, Roxie?"

"He knows better," Roxie assured him with a laugh. "We've been married too many years. Besides, he knows no one else would put up with me. Nah, he just wants to eat his dinner earlier. The man can't live on love alone."

"Ah, Roxie, why can't I find a single lady who will be as devoted to me as you are to your husband?"

Roxie smiled as she pulled into the wide driveway, part of which Jase shared with the blond neighbor next door. She stopped the car near his kitchen door, where they had a view of his wide backyard. "Hey, your vegetable garden looks great."

"Come on into the yard and take a look at it."

She hesitated only a moment. "Hey, what's another few minutes? Actually, my teenage son is getting to be a pretty good cook since I come home late so much."

They climbed out of the car and walked to the expansive garden stretching along the back fence for the width of the lot. Rows of tiny new plants stood erect in weed-free soil, and strawberry plants dotted a terraced corner at one end. The fence was topped with a sprinkler post that watered the entire garden.

"You've really gotten a lot done here in a short time, Jase. Don't you ever sleep?"

"I love working out in the fresh air and sunshine. I moved in so late in the growing season that I put the garden in before I even unpacked. I wish I could spend more time outdoors, but there's always something to do at the stores."

"Listen, better to put in the long hours of hard work to build the business while you're still young and single. On the other hand, boss," she suggested in a less than subtle tone, "you could give the people who work for you more responsibility to get the jobs done without micro-managing everything yourself."

"Is that a thinly veiled suggestion that I might not have to have my floury fingers in every pot?"

The smile slipped from her face. "Seriously, Jase. It's the mother instinct in me, I guess. I'm worried about you. There's no reason in the world why you have to be the sub for the night bakers on vacations. Hire someone else to do that so you can sleep nights. Your days at the main office are hectic enough without staying up most of the night."

"But Roxie, baking is how I got started. I love it. In fact, I miss it. I truly enjoy getting my hands into the dough again. I can knead all my cares away for a few hours." He turned and they strolled back to the driveway. "As the owner of the chain, my bakeries have to come first in my life right now. And with the sixth shop under construction, I have no right to have any free time, do I?"

Roxie shook her head. "So on top of everything else, you have the grand opening to think about and plan."

"Yeah, but once I select the promotions company I want to handle it, they can take it from there."

"Well, Wilson says the proposals are coming in. At least you'll have several to pick from."

Roxie looked around at the other nearby houses. One- and two-story structures, they were nicely kept and neatly landscaped with well-trimmed lawns. Built around the curved road, pairs of houses shared one forked driveway from the curb; each branch led to a garage behind the house.

"This is a nice area, but not where I expected you to buy," she admitted openly.

"Nothing big or showy, which is exactly why I picked it. Well-built homes that should increase in value. If anyone asks, that's why I bought here." He glanced at Roxie. "Don't you dare ask."

"Don't ask what?"

"Don't ask why I really bought a modest home in a quiet, newly built, small-town residential district instead of staying in that expensive over-decorated condo in Syracuse."

Roxie laughed. "I've worked for you since you opened your first bakery, boss. I think I can guess. You didn't downsize in style to save money. I know that, and I'm not blind." She looked around and then back at him. "This looks like a very comfortable hideout."

Jase chuckled. "You're very perceptive. That's what makes you such a good assistant." He stopped walking and turned to her. "But you've got to promise me you won't ever tell anyone around here I own the Dutch Treats bakeries. If asked, I'm just going to say I work there. Then I can only hope no one ever pays enough attention to find out the truth. With any luck, I can live in peaceful anonymity."

"But with your charity contributions and involvement in civic projects, how are you going to stay outside the limelight? People in this neighborhood must read the newspaper."

"I'll keep my name and face out of the newspapers," Jase said with a shrug.

"I don't know. I hate to see a nice, honest guy like you start out in a new neighborhood with a lie. That isn't at all like you."

"I'm not telling a lie. I'm just not telling the whole

truth." He waved his hand to dismiss the problem. "It's not as if it's going to matter to anyone."

Roxie shrugged but didn't look convinced.

"This is the kind of neighborhood I grew up in, and I think this is the one I want to live in for now."

"Well, you're the boss."

Jase shook his head. "No. Around here, I'm just a baker."

"You're not just saying that to get a rise out of me, are you?"

Jase smiled. "No way, Roxie. I knead you to be on my side."

"Even though how hard you work really frosts me? I sure hope you don't get too mixed up."

"It'll pan out," he countered, enjoying the game.

"Well, I've gotta whip on out of here."

"Well, if that's the way you want it, I can rise to the occasion and see you off."

She opened her car door. "Then I'll set my buns back in the car and roll on out of here."

"Okay, you win," Jase said, laughing at their dueling puns. "Hey, thanks again for the ride. The hassle will be diminished considerably when the renovations are finished on my car. As it is, with all the postponed deadlines, I should have rented a car. Too bad clear vision, so perfect with hindsight, isn't available ahead of time."

"Got that right. And it's too bad somebody had to steal your other car."

"I just wish they hadn't totaled it. The insurance paid me enough to get another car, but I want to see how the one the boys are renovating turns out before I decide what model to buy to go back and forth to work."

"You have all the luck! See you tomorrow." She started her car. "Oh, here. This is yours."

Jase grabbed the bag of candy she held out the window. One of his employees, who'd gotten several at a mall promotion, had handed a couple to him and Roxie as they left the store. "Thanks," he called with a wave as she drove away.

He glanced at the label on the bag as he walked to the kitchen door. "For more old-fashioned fun, call A Real Sweetie." *What a name for a candy store*, he thought. He paused on the stoop to break off a piece of hard pastel-striped ribbon candy and pop it into his mouth.

As he opened the screen, the piercing ring of a telephone sliced through the early morning silence. Realizing that the ringing was his own phone and not his cute neighbor's, he quickly dug out his house keys. But by the time he unlocked and opened the door to run in, his answering machine had picked up. His recorded voice repeated his succinct message: "This is five-five-five, two-one-one-one. Leave a message."

"Hey, sweetie, I'm up for some fun like it says here. How 'bout you?" The male caller's laugh was cut off with a click.

Jase lunged for the phone in time to hear a dial tone.

He hadn't recognized the voice, but he'd wanted to tell the jerk what he thought of the rude message.

He pressed the rewind button on the machine and noticed the number of calls received since he'd turned the machine on when he left for work the previous evening. Twenty-nine! That was a record for a phone number only his assistant knew. He couldn't help but wonder what had made him so popular all of a sudden. The tape seemed to take forever to rewind but finally began to replay.

"Hi, sweetie. Is this the number for the fun? I hope you're half as cute as the babe passing out the bags of candy in the mall."

"Get a life," Jase told the taped caller. The machine beeped and started another similar message. Jase had heard enough. He pushed aside the candy bag to turn off the machine, but his hand stopped when he saw the shiny red-and-white label on the side of the bag. He picked it up and this time read the entire label more carefully.

"For more old-fashioned fun, call A Real Sweetie at five-five-five, two-one-one-one. What? That's my phone number! No wonder I'm getting all these crank calls from men who don't even seem to know it's a candy store."

He tossed the bag on the counter and pulled the phone book from the drawer. In the business listings under "candy," he found it in black and yellow: "A Real Sweetie, an Old-Fashioned Candy Shoppe, 555-2116."

Grabbing the phone, he punched in the store's correct number and was greeted by the drone of countless unanswered rings. He dropped the phone receiver into its cradle.

Because the candy store was in one of the Syracuse malls, Jase concluded it wouldn't open until ten. After working all night on top of putting in a full day yesterday at his office, he didn't want to stay awake that long.

Jase leaned against the sink and glanced out his window as he decided what to do. His neighbor was setting up a sprinkler hose in her backyard. He'd noticed her before, stretched out in her big comfortable-looking chaise, her long legs bent to hold some papers on her lap. Maybe she was a writer.

He looked at her house and wondered what her husband did. Jase hadn't seen him once since he'd moved in. Too tired to think more about it, he turned and strode to his bedroom.

For once the sunlit hours were quiet enough for Jase to get a good day's sleep. He called the candy store that evening as soon as he was showered and dressed.

"But I'm certain the bags left in stock all have the correct phone number on them, Mr. VanDam. I have some right here on the counter in a basket. Just a minute." Jase could hear her shuffling through the paper sacks. "Yes, they all say five-five-five, two . . . Oh, dear, no!"

Jase heard her groan and knew his message had finally gotten through. "You were saying?"

"The number. The phone number on some of the bags isn't all there. It didn't print or something. Instead of a six, it looks like a one, but that's only because the loop of the six doesn't show up."

"The people calling my number don't know that. And since you just say 'old-fashioned fun,' they don't seem to know it's a candy store. But my question is, can you stop passing out the bags with the wrong number on them?"

"I assure you that I'll personally go through every bag that we have left to be sure we use only the ones with the numbers all correct."

"I guess there isn't much else I can do at this point. I appreciate your taking the time to tend to it yourself. And you'll talk to your printer soon to be sure the labels are correct before you use them next time?"

"You have my promise to take care of it right away. I don't know the printer, but I'll contact deGroot Promotions, who handles our giveaways." She clucked her tongue against the roof of her mouth. "I don't understand this happening. We used Ali's company when we first opened and never had any problems. But I'm going to call her right away to straighten this out. And I'll have her put 'candy' after 'fun' on the new ones. Let's see. I've got her number here somewhere."

Jase waited while the woman riffled through some papers. She didn't sound like an organized person. He guessed that her desk must look like a tornado had hit it.

"Yes, here's her new number. She just bought a

house outside Syracuse so she'd have enough room to run her company from home."

Jase grabbed a pen to jot the name and phone number down, but when he heard the address, he relaxed against the edge of the kitchen counter. "What was that house number?"

She repeated it. "You know where it is?"

"As a matter a fact, yes."

"Perhaps you could show your bag to Ali and let her see exactly what the difficulty is firsthand. I'll call her too, of course, but I'll probably have to leave a message. She works all hours."

"Right. Well, thanks. I'll show her my bag with the misprint. Won't be any trouble. No trouble at all." *She is just a few steps away*, he added to himself.

A big grin burst out on Jase's face as he ended the call. "So my neighbor is Ali deGroot, owner of deGroot Promotions."

He grabbed the little white bag the candy had been in, and less than twenty seconds later, he crossed their driveways and knocked on Ali's kitchen door. He waited and knocked again, but Ali never appeared. Only then did he glance into her garage and discover that her car was gone. No one else seemed to be home either. He would try again after he'd eaten dinner.

At quarter to ten that evening, Jase was leaving for work, and Ali still wasn't home. His only option was to tuck the empty candy bag above her doorknob so that his phone number, which he'd circled in red, was visible. "Wrong number," he'd written beside it. She can't miss seeing this, he thought.

His mission accomplished, for the time being at least, Jase walked out to the end of his driveway to wait for his ride to his bakery. Depending on other people or taxi drivers was getting to be a drag. He'd have to call the body shop again and lay on them about setting a date for finishing the renovations on his car.

Jase's ride arrived just as a warm June rain began to fall.

Chapter Two

Ali picked up the candy bag that fell from her door-knob as she dragged herself home after a meeting that had taken longer than she'd thought possible. That was the last time she would agree to meet a storeowner after he closed up shop for the night.

Thinking the empty candy bag had been left by the woman she'd hired to hand them out at the mall, she tossed it on the kitchen counter beside the door and headed right for bed.

The next morning she woke up late and had to rush out without breakfast. She drove through the rain that had been falling all night to the local Dutch Treats, her favorite bakery. She could get a croissant to eat on the way to her first appointment.

In the bakery's gravel parking lot, she steered around

the puddles and headed for the empty slot nearest the door. As she turned, a choked scream escaped her lips. In her peripheral vision, she saw a man exiting the store, but she saw him too late to stop. Her tire hit a pothole and sprayed a high arc of muddy rainwater right toward him.

He stood paralyzed, his gaze fixed on the spray heading his way. Ali could only watch, knowing there was no possible way he could avoid getting soaked. At the last moment he managed to raise his white bakery bag above the barrage that hit his chest full blast. He bent at the waist and uttered a cry.

In seconds it was all over. Muddy streams of water ran down his white uniform. He looked at her through the windshield and their gazes locked.

"Oh, no! Not him. Not my new neighbor," Ali croaked.

While Ali couldn't blame him one bit, she was wary of his hands, each one a fist, resting on his wet hips as he watched her park her car. She fought to free herself from her seatbelt and jumped out from behind the wheel, only to duck back in to grab a roll of paper towels she always kept under the driver's seat for emergencies.

"I'm so sorry," she said emphatically. "I didn't see the puddle there. I . . . I saw you coming out, and well . . . I guess I didn't look where I was going like I should have."

Tearing off several feet of the toweling, she crumpled it up and handed it to him. He jerked angrily at his shirt, pulling it away from his body as he leaned over, trying to shake water from the absorbent cotton but failing. She couldn't have shot him more accurately if she'd been trying with a super-sized water cannon. He rubbed at the wet marks, but the dirty water had already soaked in and wouldn't budge.

Suddenly the humor of the situation hit her. The whole scene couldn't have been more perfectly played if it had been rehearsed for a comedy movie. Now she didn't dare look up to his face—not because she was embarrassed at what she'd done, but because she was laughing so hard.

She bit her lower lip, trying to rein in her silent laughter. Just when she nearly had herself under control, she felt one of his hands cradle her jaw, gently forcing her to look directly into his face.

"Funny, huh?" A frown marred his forehead, but his gray eyes twinkled beneath his dark lashes. He was trying hard not to, but he was laughing too. Ali could no longer contain herself. She burst out laughing, and he did the same.

"This isn't how I imagined meeting my new neighbor. You could have just said hello, you know. I'm Jase VanDam." He held out his hand.

She responded with her own name and shook his hand. She was surprised how warm it felt despite the cold shower he'd just gotten. "I'm truly sorry, Jase. I'll be happy to wash your clothes and get the muddy water out."

His uniform showed the remains of a crisp, professional clean and press job. Ali couldn't imagine that a baker made a lot of money, and helping him with the cleaning bills because she'd gotten him dirty seemed to be the least she could do. "If you're heading home now, you can leave them by my kitchen door when you change. No one will bother them in our neighborhood, and I'll wash and iron them as soon as I get home tonight. You certainly shouldn't have to pay to clean the mess I made."

He didn't answer. He just stood there, looking at her rather strangely, as if she'd grown another nose on her face.

"Really. I mean it. I want to make it right," she insisted, thinking for some strange reason he didn't believe she would do that for him.

"That's all right. You must have enough laundry at home already."

"Not much laundry for one person, and I do want to undo the mess I made. Oh. Or would your wife mind?"

He looked surprised for a second and then shook his head. "Thanks, but a laundry service does all the bakery workers' whites. They can get out anything. And no, there's no wife to mind or not to mind."

He took the soiled bunches of paper towel he'd used to mop his front and tossed them in the waste can by the door. "So you live in that house next door alone too, huh?"

She nodded and shoved the roll back under her seat

as he stepped around the big puddle to her car door. "I just bought the house about a month before you bought yours. I figure it makes more sense to pay a mortgage than to waste my money on rent."

"Yeah, I agree. Say. Um . . . what brings you here to the bakery? If it wasn't just to soak me, that is?"

"No, that's not how I generally greet my new neighbors either. I wanted to get one of their yummy croissants to eat on my way to a meeting." She glanced at her watch. "Oh, no! My meeting. It's about to start without me."

"Why don't you take these cheese Danish if you want something to eat? It'll save you the time going inside." He held up the bag that had escaped the soaking and shook it.

Ali took a split second to decide it was too late to go into the shop. "Thanks. I'd hate for my stomach to growl. Not very professional," she replied with a smile.

"Your meeting wouldn't take you near our houses, would it? I was thinking maybe I could hitch a ride home."

"It won't, but the house isn't that far. Hop in. Dropping you off is no problem after giving you a muddy shower."

Jase jogged around the car and climbed in. Ali set the bakery bag between them and took out one of the rolls.

"Here, you take the other one. I'll just eat this to tide me over until after my meeting." She took a bite and chewed. "Mmm. These are so good. You'll have to tell me how you make them so light. But then, that's probably one of the company's secrets."

"If everyone could make them taste that good, Dutch Treats would go out of business," Jase replied with a grin.

Ali laughed, started the car, and drove out of the lot. "I don't know how you do it. You're around all those yummy sweets all the time and there's not a bit of extra fat on you. If I worked in a bakery, I'd be big as a house."

Jase chuckled. She glanced over to catch him scrutinizing her. "Just trying to picture you that big."

She felt heat rise into her cheeks. "There's enough butter in this to make me gain ten pounds while you watch."

"Do you eat your breakfast on the run all the time?"

"Yeah, and today this is lunch too, if things continue to go the way they have so far this morning." She put the last of the roll into her mouth and licked her fingers, aware that Jase was watching her every move.

"Then you'll have to let me take you out to dinner to make sure you get a decent meal in today."

She swallowed the last bite. "You want to take me out after the way I soaked you?"

"We don't want to harbor any bad feelings between neighbors, do we?"

"No, but that doesn't mean we have to go out to dinner."

"Um, did I misinterpret your having only laundry for one? Is there someone who would not want you to go out with me?"

"No!" she said emphatically. She glanced at him and saw that he was surprised by her vehement denial. "There's no one," she added in a more normal voice.

"You're sure about that?" he joked.

"I'm sure. There used to be, but not long enough ago to forget my anger, I guess. And what about you?"

"Nope, no one," he said with a grin. "So what about dinner? You never know, we might actually have fun."

Ali pulled down their street. "I guess it would be okay. But I insist on paying for my own meal. After all, you've already treated me to breakfast. There's no reason for you to take me to dinner too."

"Actually, I can't literally take you. My car was totaled a few weeks ago and my other car is in the garage being fixed up. It won't be ready for another week or two. So I was hoping you could drive."

"Sure. I can't imagine being without a car." Ali pulled into his side of the driveway and stopped short of his kitchen door. She turned to him, waiting for him to get out of her car.

"I have a lot of friends at work who have kindly offered me rides so I didn't have to rent a car. So, is it a date for dinner then?"

"No, not a date. It's just two neighbors eating together, remember?" She looked out the windshield so she could avoid looking at his gorgeous smile. Each time she saw it, her stomach felt as if a whole flock of hummingbirds were fluttering around inside it.

"Not a date?"

She shook her head. She wasn't going to add herself to the long list of woman she'd seen him coming or going with in the short time he'd lived next door. Appearing at all sorts of odd hours, they couldn't all just be giving him rides.

"Okay, we'll do it your way. Thanks for the ride. See you about seven?"

"That'll be fine."

After carefully backing out of the driveway, Ali raced to her meeting but couldn't concentrate on her agenda. She kept thinking about the tall Dutchman with a gorgeous smile that didn't seem to quit.

Ali clicked "save" on her computer and reached for the phone on the second ring. "deGroot Promotions."

"Hi. It's Jase. I'm sorry, but I have to get to the bakery in time to close up at seven this evening. The manager had to take care of a family emergency, so now I can't meet you for dinner because I'll have to start baking after I'm done closing up. I hate to, but I'm afraid I'm going to have to postpone our 'non-date' evening together."

Startled by how disappointed she felt, Ali frowned. "I understand, Jase. Hey, look at it this way. You're earning extra overtime hours. They'll look good on your paycheck."

"What? Oh, sure. Well, I'll talk to you soon and we can reschedule. Okay?"

Maybe he regretted canceling too, she thought with a smile as she agreed and hung up the phone to get back to work.

It wasn't until she was tidying up the kitchen later after eating a sandwich for supper that she noticed the candy bag she'd tossed on the counter the night before. An inked circle on the label drew her attention. She took a closer look at the bag and saw the incorrect phone number. She groaned. That explained the messages to call the candy store.

"That printer has gotten me in trouble this time. I work long and hard, and then something stupid like this has to happen," she ranted aloud to herself.

Using her office phone, she called A Real Sweetie. This time she caught the owner.

"Sorry I was out when you called before. I wanted to tell you about the bag labels, but I guess you found out the problem on your own, 'cause the guy who called said he would stop by."

"Whoever has this misprinted phone number must be really annoyed if they came all the way to my house to leave the bag for me to see."

"He seemed nice enough on the phone," the owner told her. "At least, I don't think we need to worry that he's badmouthing the store. Which is not to say we don't have a problem, of course. I'm guessing twenty percent of the labels we have left in the store were printed poorly enough to make the phone number look wrong."

"That many?" Ali squeaked. "I'll call the printer right away and get new correct ones."

"I'd like to add the word 'candy' after 'fun' too. The man who called suggested that and it works for me."

"You'll need them to put candy in for customers in the store, but I think we should stop handing them out if they result in this many crank calls, even with the word 'candy' added."

"One promotion using them was enough and I do have several new customers already, so that's good. By the way, I gave the guy your address as well as your phone number since your office is in your house, but I got to thinking about it. With you living alone, Ali, maybe I shouldn't have. Nowadays you never know. I'd hate to be responsible for some kook showing up at your door."

"It's okay. He just left a bag on my doorknob. At least we both have his phone number." She laughed. "But I'm sure there won't be a problem with his knowing where to find me. I'll call him to apologize and smooth things over. I just hope he's not still getting a lot of annoying calls."

"Maybe he'd give me his phone number to use for a second phone line, and he could get a new one. I need all the calls I can get," the storeowner replied with a chuckle.

"I'll see what I can work out," Ali responded in kind.

She wished her a good day and called the printer. He was apologetic and willing to make new corrected labels by the next day.

"I'll be sure to watch the ink level," he promised.

"And you'll check on your quality control system? I can't use you if mistakes like these get by, especially not in this quantity."

He agreed, and Ali then dialed the wrong number on the bag. After ten rings she decided the individual must be at work. She'd try again later in the evening.

Next she dialed her sister, Helen, at her condo home near Chicago. Except for Helen's sometimes annoying matchmaking efforts, they'd grown closer since their parents' accidental deaths, soon after Helen had gotten married. When Jeff deceived her and walked out, Ali didn't know what she would have done without her sister's support and frequent understanding phone calls.

"I'm glad you called," Helen told her. "You seem to know just when I can use a line to the outside world."

"Maybe it just happens to be when I need the line too."

"You're so self-contained and working so hard on your business that if you want to talk, it's either because business is slipping or you've met a man."

"My business is good and keeping me so busy I can't find enough time to eat."

"Then tell me all about him."

Ali laughed. "You never give up, do you? Yes, I met a man, but he's not my Mr. Right. He's my neighbor. A baker. He's the one I told you works at all sorts of odd hours."

"The hunk next door? He's not married?"

"No, but before your matchmaking tendencies take over, Helen, you should know I've rarely seen him with the same woman more than twice. He must have a really great line that he feeds them."

"What do you mean?" Helen asked.

"Well, his car is being fixed and he seems to be able to talk women into driving him to and from work each day."

Helen whistled low and long. "I can't wait to meet this Mr. Not Right."

"Not much chance of that. We were supposed to go to dinner, but he backed out at the last minute."

"Didn't he have a good excuse?"

"I suppose. He had to work."

"He sounds responsible. I still want to meet him next time I come out there."

"Do I dare introduce you, or will you embarrass me and try to fix us up?"

"I'll behave, I promise," Helen replied, laughing.

Ali laughed. "That'll be the day."

"Ouch. Am I that bad?"

"Let's just say you don't give up on your goal of getting me married, but I do like talking to you. You can always make me laugh. But forget about my neighbor and let me tell you about a mistake my printer made. Then you can cheer me up all over again."

* * *

"This is not A Real Sweetie," a gruff-voiced man said the next morning when Ali dialed the wrong number yet again and finally got an answer.

The printing error must have been a bigger problem for him than she'd hoped. Silence followed the unfriendly announcement except for the noise of the man biting into what sounded like a potato chip. Potato chips for breakfast?

"Hello?" Ali cleared her throat. "Ah, I know you're not the candy store. I've called to apologize for what looks like your phone number appearing on some of the candy store bags. I've learned from the storeowner that you've been getting calls because of the printing error, and I want you to know that I am very sorry that you were inconvenienced. Ah . . ."

The guy sure wasn't making this easy for her. He didn't say a word.

"I've already called the printer," Ali said into the silence. "Yesterday, in fact. I couldn't reach you earlier, and I wanted you to know that they're already printing new stickers for the store to use. We've destroyed all the remaining ones with the phone number that looks like yours. Ah . . . I hope you haven't been pestered by a lot of calls."

"Dozens."

That voice. Ali frowned, trying to place it with a face. It wasn't easy to do because she met so many people in her job. "Well, I won't take any more of your time. I just wanted you to know that I truly regret that you were bothered."

"Apology accepted."

"Oh, no. It can't be you," she whispered. Her heart-beat sped up so that she heard its pounding in the ear-piece of the phone. Clutching the receiver with both hands, she swallowed hard.

"Ali?"

"Jase, it *is* you. Why didn't you tell me? You received dozens of annoying calls because of my promotion, but you didn't say a word yesterday about the mistake on the candy bags."

"Hey, you soaked me with muddy water when I hadn't done a thing, I was afraid of what you might do if I complained," Jase joked.

Ali laughed. "But you had every right to be furious and you were so . . . so nice."

"Hey. What can I say? There's a lot more to me than meets the eye."

"Jase, I am so sorry. Were there really that many calls?"

"Yeah, but not so many after the first night when your people were passing the bags out in the mall."

"The ad campaign didn't get the results we wanted with you getting crank calls."

"Yeah, now I unplug the phone most of the time. I just plugged it in this morning while I ate. I'm glad I did because you were the one to call."

"Now I understand. While it was unplugged, I kept getting no answer. Oh, but your breakfast. I'm sorry to interrupt."

"No problem. I'm just eating cinnamon-bread toast. Love that stuff toasted really crispy."

"Then you weren't eating potato chips."

"For breakfast?"

"I thought I heard . . . Never mind, your toast is getting cold."

"Don't stop talking on my account. I'm in no hurry."

"No, I must. I mean, you worked all night, so you need your rest."

"Nice to know I'm living in an area where neighbors care about neighbors."

"Sweet dreams, Jase." Ali set the phone in the cradle and laid her hand flat across her belly. The hummingbirds were back, fluttering around even more than last time.

Jase hung up the phone and finished his breakfast. At first, it had felt odd coming home from work and eating eggs and toast instead of a steak, but when he worked nights, breakfast just made sense. He put his plate in the dishwasher and wiped up the counter where he'd sliced the cinnamon bread.

He was preoccupied with his thoughts, and by the time he was ready to climb into bed, he still hadn't stopped thinking about Ali. The women he'd dated, the ones who flocked around him because they were attracted to his money, had never interested him as Ali did.

Jase sat up in bed. He suddenly realized he wanted to see her again. To date her and get to know more about her. Just to be with her. He wanted to grab the chance to be with a woman who might be attracted to him—not to his money or his stores. He smiled and plopped back down on the pillow.

Moving to this small suburb had been the right choice. He could protect his anonymity . . . and have fun with his spunky neighbor.

All he had to do was lie about himself. Well, he rationalized immediately, it wasn't exactly lying. She'd already assumed he was a night baker at the shop, and he just wouldn't correct her erroneous conclusion. He'd have to figure out a better description of what he did at the office where he worked most days, but maybe not. It wasn't likely she'd ask him the same question again.

His relationship to the bakeries shouldn't have anything to do with taking her out. He would do his best to keep her from finding out. It wouldn't be all that tough, and it appeared to be well worth it. He didn't want to spoil any of the fun they could have together.

"Besides, one little white lie couldn't do any harm," he reiterated as he rolled over to get some sleep.

Chapter Three

Stepping outside, Ali closed her kitchen door and locked the deadbolt. Dressed in jeans and a knit top, she was glad she had a jacket on, as the morning air felt cool after the overnight rain. She raised her purse strap to her shoulder and turned off the stoop onto the driveway.

She carried a small collapsible umbrella as insurance against more rain, despite the mostly clear sky that the weather forecaster said meant no rain for the next hour or two. Hoping that would be the case, she crossed the asphalt surface toward her garage, where her car was already loaded with all she would need. Never one to leave anything to the last minute, she'd loaded all the signs and props the night before.

A tapping on Jase's kitchen window stopped her. She looked up to see him holding up one index finger. "Wait a minute," he called through the glass before he disappeared. Dressed in jeans and a sweatshirt, he opened his side door moments later. Picking his way carefully so he didn't step on a stone with his bare feet, he crossed their shared end of the driveway to her.

"Good morning," she said. Funny how her heart began to race as he neared, she thought.

"I'm glad I caught you. I just heard a weather forecast. It's supposed to clear up. I saw you out here and wondered if you would like to drive up to Oneida Lake. I have the day off and we could nose around and get that dinner we missed at one of the restaurants along the shore. You game?"

Ali smiled. "That sounds like so much fun, but I can't go today. I have a big display to set up in the mall. I have to have it finished by tonight for a sale that starts tomorrow. Thanks, though."

She turned her back to Jase and continued the route to her car so he couldn't see the disappointment she was certain must be showing on her face.

"See ya," he called as he turned to walk back into his house. "Wait!" he shouted suddenly. "Listen, about our dinner."

"It's okay, Jase. Really," she said, thinking he'd changed his mind about wanting to take her out.

As she turned to face him again, he stepped on a rock. With a yelp, he raised one foot and brushed at the bottom while balancing on the other.

"No, wait. I mean I still want very much to go to

dinner with you. What about Wednesday night? Can we go then?"

She pondered his question as she tried to picture her schedule on her calendar. "I can't think of any reason why not."

He lowered his foot to stand on it. "Good. I'll make a reservation for seven. I know just the perfect place." Turning, he picked his way back to his door but stopped and looked at her when she spoke.

"Since you have a particular place in mind, should I dress in a special way?"

Grinning with that gorgeous smile of his, he shook his head. "Whatever you wear is fine. Actually, I've seen everything there from jeans to suits, but not many of the latter."

"Sounds good." She glanced at her watch. "I gotta go." He smiled at her as she jogged the few feet left to her car. Her steps felt lighter than they had in some time.

By Wednesday, Ali had selected and rejected a dozen wardrobe combinations to wear to dinner with Jase. Reluctantly answering her phone whenever it rang, she'd half expected him to call and cancel again, but he hadn't. Decision time came and she pulled on linen slacks and a silk blouse. She carried a sweater in case she needed it later in the evening.

She was in the kitchen ready to go when Jase knocked on her door. When she opened the door, the smile on his face told her she'd picked the right outfit.

She'd left her car out that afternoon, so in minutes she had locked up her house and they were on the way to the restaurant.

She hadn't been able to spend the day with him on a lake, but he'd chosen a restaurant where they could spend the evening looking at one while they ate. They were shown right to their table.

Ali sat in the chair Jase pulled out for her at the linen-covered table. She set her purse on the chair to her left and leaned over to smell the fresh freesia in the vase near her plate while Jase sat down opposite her.

"I'm glad our schedules meshed enough to finally have our dinner together," Jase said as they each laid their napkins over their laps. "I kept my fingers crossed all day."

"I know, and I bet it was hard to work with your fingers crossed that way," she said, unable to keep a straight face.

"Would I use an old joke like that to amuse you?" he asked with feigned innocence.

Ali laughed but could only nod because the waitress arrived at their table. "This restaurant is wonderful. I hope the food is as good as the views of Skaneateles Lake," Ali volunteered after they had ordered and the waitress had left with their menus.

"I still want to take you to Oneida." Jase looked out at the lake. "It's too bad the dining room doesn't face west. We could watch the sunset."

"All that good New York air pollution does give us some pretty ones," Ali replied.

The waitress brought their colorful salads. Ali spooned on a little of the dressing. "This looks delicious. I never have this many different vegetables in my refrigerator at the same time."

"Yeah," he agreed. "Cooking for one never excited me."

"You know, the Dutch Treats rolls are better than these," she said, holding up a limp one from the basket.

"You sound like a loyal customer."

"I love the bakery where you work. I go there all the time. Maybe I should suggest that this restaurant's buyer go over to one of the stores."

Jase laughed. "I should hire you . . . I mean, of course, the bakery should hire you as a salesman," he said. He leaned back in his chair. "Enough about the bakeries. Tell me about you. Were you raised in this area?"

A small frown creased her brow. "You really don't like to talk about yourself and the bakery you work for, huh?"

Jase shrugged. "I'd rather learn about you."

"But I can't get over that I've been shopping in that same bakery for weeks and I don't remember seeing you there before."

"I just got lucky now, I guess, but let's not talk about work. We're here to enjoy ourselves."

Jase straightened in his chair and looked out the window. If talking about work made him look uncomfortable, she would steer clear of the subject, he thought.

"I think if I had a view like that to look at all the

time, I would never get any work done," Ali told him, changing the subject herself instead of waiting for him to do it. "I would just be watching the water and all the activity on and around it."

Dusk was settling in as the waitress placed their dinners before them.

"You know, it occurred to me," Ali ventured. "You never get to see much of the sun working nights and sleeping days."

Jase chuckled. "I don't work nights very often. I've just been working odd nights lately to replace people who are on vacation. Most of the time I work days in the Syracuse office."

"That's a long commute. What do you do at the office?"

"Um . . . a little of this. A little of that. One of the things I like best is creating new recipes."

She tried to picture him working in a test kitchen at the headquarters building. He was probably working his way up the ladder at Dutch Treats, Ali concluded. "And to think that I thought being a baker would be boring because you had to do the same thing over and over. Oops! Here I am, still talking about work. Sorry."

They ate for a while in companionable silence.

"These sautéed vegetables are done to perfection," Ali put in. "Keeping fresh ones in the fridge requires frequent trips to the grocery store that I don't always have time for."

"Mmm. One of the reasons I bought the house was to

have a yard to work in. I love eating fresh vegetables, and I enjoy being able to work out there nearly every weekend."

"I find I *have* to work in the yard that often just to keep up with it, and all I have to work on is the lawn and the landscaping around the foundation. I'm glad I don't work nights like you do. I couldn't stay awake during the day to get anything done."

"I have an enormous vegetable garden along the fence in the backyard, but I guess you know that. Anyway, you're welcome to some vegetables for a more varied salad like the one you ate here tonight."

"Thanks. Right neighborly of you," she teased. "But only if you have extra. More than you need, I mean. I've seen you out there, weeding early in the morning and sometimes after dinnertime in the evening—in addition to the weekends. You've worked so hard, you deserve to eat everything that grows there."

"A garden does take a lot of time, but I love to work outside," he replied.

Ali shook her head and waited until the waitress had cleared their dishes. "I don't know how you manage. How can you arbitrarily change your sleep cycle so often?"

Jase shrugged. "It's a crazy schedule, but not too unlike your own, I might add."

"But I couldn't keep changing it constantly from night to day and back like you do. I may stay up very late working occasionally, but at least I sleep the rest of the nights, and I can sleep in a morning or two to catch up once in a while."

Ali looked up and her gaze locked with his. She suddenly realized just how much they'd been watching each other. They even knew each other's schedules. She looked down at her napkin and raised it to touch the corners of her mouth.

"You folks all finished?" the waitress asked, bringing Ali out of her reverie.

She and Jase declined coffee, and the waitress placed the bill in its plastic folder on the table. Despite an initial objection from Jase, they amicably paid the bill by splitting it in half.

Outside, Jase took a gentle hold of her bent elbow to stop her as they walked to her car. "Let's walk down to the lake for a few minutes. The path and the dock are well lit."

"Sure," Ali replied with a smile.

Keeping his hand on her elbow, he guided her down the cinder path to the shore. They saw only one boat still on the water, its white, red, and green lights shining brightly as it pulled into a dock.

"You know, you didn't have to pay for your own dinner, Ali. I asked you out," Jase said.

"Hey, I thought you'd like the practice of Dutch treat."

Jase laughed. "No pun intended, I'll bet," he said.

Swatting at a mosquito near her forehead first, Ali was quickly busy swatting at others. Jase dropped his hand from her arm to slap one on the back of his neck.

"Guess this evening walk by the water wasn't a good idea," he said, laughing. "Come on."

With a stronger grip on her other arm, he urged her to run as quickly as she could in her low heels. He opened the car door for her and quickly ran around to his side when she was settled. A little breathless, they laughed.

"That's the closest I've felt to being something's dinner," Ali claimed. "Must be all those sweet Dutch treats we eat."

Jase dispatched a mosquito that had managed to get into the car with them. Ali pulled out of the parking lot and headed home. They talked easily as she, spurred on by Jase's questions, described what her promotions business did for companies. He laughed heartily about the funnier incidents at some of the giveaways she had staged.

"You know, this evening has been fun. I've been all work and no play lately. I'm glad you suggested dinner, Jase. It was delicious," Ali said as they climbed from her car.

"What? No invitation to come in for coffee?"

"This isn't a date, remember?"

He dramatically hit his forehead with his palm. "How could I forget?" He stepped closer, making her tilt her head back to maintain the connection between their gazes. "And if this is not a date, I can't kiss you good night, I suppose."

Ali looked at him with a surprised wide-eyed look.

"Kiss me? Jase, that isn't a good idea." She turned away, happy to have the excuse of closing the automatic garage door.

"I'd have to take exception to that conclusion, Ali. Personally, I think it's a great idea." He walked beside her to her kitchen door.

"But we're neighbors. We have to get along in order to live next door to each other. That would be easier if we didn't have a close personal relationship."

"I'd say we're getting along real well. I had a great time tonight."

She had to laugh at that observation. "So did I, but you know what I mean."

He shook his head and raised his hand to gently rub her cheek with the back of his knuckles. "No, I'm afraid I don't."

She looked down, unable to meet his gaze. "Then let's just agree that I'm not the kind of woman you're probably used to. I haven't dated since my engagement blew up in my face. And if I did date you, I would never . . . well, never mind what I don't do. I'm just not your type."

Tipping her chin up with a bent finger, forcing her to meet his gaze again, Jase stared at her for a few moments. "I haven't discussed what my type of woman is with you, so shouldn't you let me decide that?" he asked softly.

"But . . ."

"But you needn't worry. I'm not one to rush into anything. Let's just get to know each other. And for now, you can have it your way. No good-night kiss."

He backed across the driveway, their gazes still locked. Then he broke the fragile connection between them and went inside.

Ali stepped into her kitchen and closed the door, sagging against it. "Refusing that kiss may have been the dumbest thing I did all day," she whispered.

Chapter Four

That Saturday, Ali felt quite proud of herself. She was all caught up on her promotions work and actually had the afternoon free to work in her yard. With little regard to how muddy the knees of her jeans were getting, she had banished every weed she could find in the mulched landscaping around her house and along the garage. Her rechargeable electric mower had trimmed the grass nicely, chewing up the lush green blades and sending them flying.

Pausing before she pushed the mower from the front lawn back into the garage, she took a moment to admire her own work. *Looking good*, she thought. *Yeah, buying this house was definitely a good idea.*

As she pushed the mower up the driveway, a car pulled in behind her on Jase's side. Ali glanced over her shoulder to see Jase climb out the passenger side and shut the door.

"Thanks, Roxie," he called.

"No problem, boss." The woman driving appeared to be fifty-ish. She waved over the steering wheel and backed out to go on her way.

Ali thought "boss" was a strange nickname for a night baker, but then, Jase was tall and commanding in appearance, and he did spend a lot of time at the bakery. Given his sense of humor, she could see how someone might jokingly call him that.

"Working hard, I see," he said, following her into the garage. "The yard looks great."

"Thanks." Sliding the mower into place, she attached the electrical cable. "Just finished," she said as she pulled off her floral cotton gardening gloves.

"Great. We can both get cleaned up and get a pizza and maybe take in a movie. How does that sound?" he asked with a grin. "Of course, it isn't a date," he added, holding up his hand, palm toward her. "No, it's just two neighbors spending a few hours together."

Ali shook her head with a laugh and tossed her work gloves on the workbench. "Unaccustomed as I am to making snap decisions, that sounds great. After working all afternoon, I wasn't looking forward to having to make dinner too."

"Meet you right here in half an hour?" He stepped backwards toward his door but stopped and frowned.

"Or are you one of those women who takes forever and a day to shower and get dressed?"

She laughed. "Hey! There's a reason I wear my hair short. Make that twenty-eight minutes!" Taking off at a run, she disappeared into her house.

Jase laughed and headed for his own shower. He thought of the other women he'd dated lately and knew that not one of them could shower and dress in twenty-eight minutes. Not even close to that. Part of the reason Ali could was that she wore so little makeup. She didn't need more. Her skin glowed with an inner beauty and energy that was fresh and exciting.

Energized, he jogged down the hall to his bedroom. After her boast, he didn't dare take more than the allotted time. Showered and changed, he heard her shut her door as he was locking his own.

"Piece of cake," she said with a grin, vertically sweeping her hands past each other as if dusting off flour. "Twenty-eight minutes on the dot, and my shoes match too." She lifted her slacks a couple of inches and wiggled her toes in the open sandals.

They laughed and joked all evening. Ali was fun to spend time with. No pretence. None of the trying to make an impression he'd felt in other women. With Ali, what he saw was what he got. He liked that. Liked it a lot.

At the popcorn counter in the movie theater, Jase asked, "Small or large popcorn?"

"Are you going to eat any of it?" she asked with a grin.

"I sure hope so. You can't watch a movie without popcorn."

"That's exactly how I see it. We'd better get a large, but this is my treat. You wouldn't let me pay for my half of the pizza." She pulled her shoulder bag forward and reached for her wallet.

Jase closed his hand over hers. "Tonight is all my treat," he said softly. "Besides, you didn't eat half the pizza."

"But you don't need to buy everything."

"I know, Ali. But I want to."

"But I . . ."

They had reached the counter, where a young man in a paper hat asked what they wanted. Jase kept his hand around Ali's and pulled it off her purse, giving her no choice but to let him pay.

As they waited for their large popcorn and two sodas, a woman passing Jase suddenly grabbed his arm. "Jase! Jase VanDam. How come you've made yourself so scarce lately?"

"We know you moved out, but you could come visit us once in a while, you know," her friend beside her said. Her lower lip was extended in a big pout. "We miss you."

Jase clenched his teeth as he turned around. "Tami, Geri," he said, nodding to each of them. "Ah, Ali, these women were my neighbors where I used to live."

"Oh, nice to meet you," Ali said with a smile. She

started to extent her hand to the women, but they had already turned their attention solely to Jase.

"Here's your popcorn and soda, mister," the boy behind the counter called, interrupting their questions about where Jase lived now.

"Right," Jase said, turning to the counter and paying for them. He handed Ali one of the sodas. Holding the popcorn barrel against his chest with one arm, he gripped Ali's elbow with his free hand and urged her toward the turnstile. "Enjoy your movie," he said over his shoulder to the women still watching them.

"Hey, don't run away," Tami insisted as she tugged on his sleeve. "We're having a party tomorrow night and we want you to come." She looked at Ali and added, as an afterthought, "You could come too, I suppose."

Jase could hardly believe that he used to find these women attractive. Sure, they had knockout figures clothed in the latest fashion. Any movie star would be happy to be made up as carefully as they were. But Ali had more class in her little finger than both of them had in their whole bodies.

"Thanks, but I have to work," he said to shut them up.

"Oh, sure. You've got to work on Sunday. I'll just bet you do, boss-man," Geri put in with a laugh.

"Lady, do you want something or not?" the boy behind the counter asked Tami.

"What? Oh, yeah," Jase heard her reply as he made his escape with Ali.

That had been too close for Jase's comfort. It was the

second time someone had called him "boss" in front of Ali. She hadn't said anything, but he had to wonder what she was thinking about it.

"Our movie is about to start," he insisted as they hurried down the wide, carpeted hall.

Jase had a hard time concentrating on the movie. He was too busy mentally kicking himself. Not telling Ali who he was hadn't seemed like a big deal before. It was just a little lie, but he was very uncomfortable at the prospect of telling her so long after meeting her.

Now it was a big deal and getting bigger by the day.

And now he knew that he didn't want anything to threaten their blossoming relationship.

"I can't believe you'll be here tomorrow," Ali said excitedly when Helen called the next week.

"Let's just say I have cabin fever so bad that I have to get out. You don't mind that I come on such short notice?"

"Heavens, no. I've wanted you to come for weeks, but isn't Eric due home soon?"

"He left very quickly and didn't know when he'd be back. It could still be weeks more, and the more that happens in the Middle East near where he's working on that well, the more I worry about him. It would be easier to wait for him to come home if I was with you. Besides, I used one of those websites and found a last-minute cheap airfare that I couldn't refuse."

"Fantastic. I can't wait for you to get here."

"Is the airport far for you to pick me up?"

"Not at all. I'll be out front," Ali promised.

"No problem. I'll find you."

On her way to the airport the next morning, Ali made a quick stop at the Dutch Treats bakery to get rolls for their breakfast. When she returned to her car, she was surprised to see Jase leaning casually against the front fender.

"We've got to stop meeting like this in a parking lot," he said dramatically.

Ali laughed. "I hate to disappoint you, but I didn't come here to meet you."

"Darn. I thought you missed me," he said, affecting an exaggerated pout.

"Sorry, neighbor. I know it's tough to take, but I just came for the bakery goodies, not you," she teased as she set the box of sweet rolls she'd just bought on the center of the front seat.

"Looks like you bought enough for a crowd. Did I miss seeing my invitation to breakfast at your house this morning?"

Ali laughed. "I guess I did buy a lot, but I'm on my way to pick up my sister at the airport. I thought I'd treat us both to your yummy breakfast rolls." She climbed in and closed the door of her car, but opened the window to continue the conversation when Jase showed no signs of moving away.

"Your sister's coming for a visit?"

"Yeah. I haven't seen her in ages, but I've been really busy with painting and decorating the house on top of working at earning a living all day."

"So you're planning to go right home after you pick up your sister at the airport?"

"That's the plan. She hasn't seen my house yet. I can't wait to show it to her."

"Great," Jase said with a ready grin, running around the car to the opposite door. "You can give me a lift home." He climbed in and fastened his seat belt. "Is there a problem with that?" he asked when she didn't move.

Ali shook her head. "Did anyone ever tell you you're pushy? No wonder your friends call you 'boss.' "

"Pushy? Well, maybe, but never annoying," he said solemnly after a few seconds. "I promise."

"And I'm supposed to believe what you tell me about yourself? A likely story," Ali said with a laugh to show she was joking.

He didn't keep the light-hearted banter going. As she waited to pull out into the street, she glanced over at him. He was watching her, but he wasn't grinning. Just a bit of a smile curled up the corners of his lips. He really didn't like talking about himself, she surmised.

"Thanks for the ride, neighbor. I do appreciate it. That you can believe," he said softly.

Ali laughed at his serious demeanor. Hadn't he known she was joking? "I never doubted for a minute that I could believe anything you told me."

"Yeah. Right," he said strangely.

Ali had no time to figure out what he meant before he swung his hand up to cover his mouth as it opened wide in a yawn. He shut his eyes and leaned his head back against the headrest with a big sigh.

Ali turned her attention back to driving and let him relax. He had to be tired after working all night again. As they arrived at the Syracuse airport, twenty minutes later, Jase hadn't stirred or spoken. She maneuvered into the correct terminal lane and glanced over at him. He was asleep.

He looked vulnerable and exposed. Ali hadn't thought about it before, but sleeping in the presence of someone else was a very trusting thing to do. She smiled, happy to think that he trusted her and felt he could act so naturally around her.

That's what she hoped to find in her Mr. Right someday. Honesty and trust, with no deception.

She noticed that he needed a shave. The dark shadow of his stubble contributed to his rugged handsomeness. Ali frowned. He had to be very tired to fall asleep in her car. Worried anew about him, she hoped his health wasn't suffering from the long hours he worked. To her, earning more money wasn't worth endangering one's health.

"Jase, we're at the airport," she said softly enough to wake but not startle him. "Wake up, Jase," she said more loudly. "I understand that you've been working all night at the bakery and you're tired, but it won't look good to have you asleep in my car. My sister has a very active imagination. Runs in the family, I guess."

He groaned softly and resettled himself, covering a yawn with his hand without opening his eyes.

"I guess I'm funny that way, but I'd like Helen to get to know you as my neighbor and not as someone who appears to have passed out in the front seat next to me."

Getting no further reaction from him, she grasped his muscular arm below the rolled-up white sleeve and gave him a little shake. "Jase?" The hairs on his arm tickled the palm of her hand.

His eyes blinked open and he smiled lazily at her as he laid his hand over hers and squeezed it a moment before she pulled it away. "I'm awake, but I'm sure you'd figure out something to tell your sister," he mumbled. "You have a great imagination yourself, and besides, it might be fun to hear your explanation."

Ali pulled up to the curb in front of the baggage claim and cut the engine. "Uh, speaking of Helen." Ali worried what Helen would say when she saw Jase. She needed to warn him.

"Her name's Helen?"

"Yes, and . . . uh, I have to tell you that she may get a little excited when she meets you. It's not about you, or anything." She shook her head. "Well, actually it is about you, but it's all in her head."

"Would you swing that by me once more?" he asked with a frown as he straightened in his seat.

Ali sighed and met his gaze. "Well, I mentioned to her on the phone that I'd met the man who'd moved in next door to me, and I know she read a lot into that simple statement—especially when I told her you were single and good-looking."

"Good-looking?" He grinned. "You think I'm good-looking?"

She felt her cheeks warm but ignored his question. "Anyway, I just wanted to tell you about this annoying trait of hers so you'd understand."

He grinned, putting her at ease at once. She leaned back on the headrest and looked out the windshield at the passengers coming out of the terminal.

"Helen can pump up our simple friendship into a story in which we would be heading to a wedding chapel any second. Which of course, we're not."

"No, of course not," he said softly enough for Ali to glance over and see the big grin on his face.

Quickly looking away, she toyed with the steering wheel. "She hasn't always been that way. After I discovered my fiancé wasn't what he appeared to be, Helen felt really bad. Back then she left me alone for a while, but now she wants to fix me up every chance she gets. She's completely convinced I'll be much happier married."

His smile disappeared and Jase looked at her strangely. She couldn't blame him. He was in for the full treatment when Helen got to the car.

"Do you want to tell me more of what happened to end your engagement?"

Ali stared out the windshield. She hated talking about Jeff. She waited to feel her stomach ache and her cheeks warm with the embarrassment at having been so gullible, the anger at being cheated and stolen from . . . but it wasn't like that this time. Startled, she looked at Jase, who met her gaze, patiently waiting.

"It's not easy for me to tell what happened. He . . ." She swallowed against the lump in her throat. "I found out he'd deceived me about . . . ah . . . who he was and what he'd done. We'd planned to get married, and for nearly a year before the wedding date, we both put money into a bank account to save for a house down payment and furniture. I went to make a deposit about a month before we . . . before the scheduled wedding and . . ."

She had to breathe deeply to be able to continue. "He'd taken all the money out of the account except for the minimum the bank needed to keep it open. I guess he didn't want me to find out until he'd made his getaway. A whole year of my savings that I'd put in the account was gone. And so was he. He disappeared and I never saw or heard from him again."

Frowning, Jase listened without saying a word.

"Anyway, I couldn't trust men after that. You're actually the first one I've even gone out with more than once." She grinned. "You must have an honest aura about you."

Her attention was drawn to a group of passengers exiting the terminal. "Hey, there are some more people. She's probably coming, but I wanted to apologize in advance for her. Helen can be really embarrassing sometimes, and I just wanted to clue you in so you wouldn't be surprised. Please don't take what she says personally, okay? I don't want you to feel as if you're in an awkward position."

He put his hand over hers on the seat between them and squeezed gently before releasing it. "Not a problem. And you never have to apologize to me for the words or actions of someone else." He chuckled. "You should hear my mother on the subject of my settling down. She always wants to know when I'm going to get married and give her the requisite two and a half grand-kids she's waiting not-at-all-patiently for."

Ali smiled as a second rush of people left the terminal building and headed across the lanes to the covered parking garage.

"It looks like a big group of passengers are coming out now. Might be her flight from Chicago."

"When was her plane due?"

"Ten minutes ago. I told her I'd park here and wait for her to come out. But I don't know how long they'll let me park here. Let's hope these people are from her plane."

"Is she blond and beautiful like you?"

"That's a laugh. Jase, she *is* the beautiful blond in the family, if that's any help. She's tall and willowy and has always made me feel like the ugly duckling sister."

"No way." Jase jumped out of the car. "There's no

way you could be the ugly duckling by any stretch of the imagination," he said before shutting the door.

Ali pushed the button that would open the window on his side of the car. "Jase. Wait. You don't need to go inside. I asked her to meet me outside the terminal."

Chapter Five

Noting the little wave over his shoulder to acknowledge that he'd heard her, Ali watched as Jase strode through the big automatic revolving doors into the building. She drew her lower lip between her teeth and worried what Helen would think. Dressed in white, Jase could be an orderly from a mental institution. She chuckled at the idea.

"Wait! You don't even know her last name to page her. It's . . ." she called suddenly, but Jase had already disappeared. She groaned and turned the key in the ignition. Stabbing the window button to keep the air-conditioned air inside her car, she welcomed the cool breeze blowing toward her face.

Tapping her thumbs on the steering wheel, she watched the glass front of the terminal for some sign of

Jase or Helen. Several minutes later she spotted Jase exiting the building with a suitcase in his hand. Helen strode in step next to him, guided by his hand protectively cupping her elbow. She was grinning broadly.

What had he said to make her laugh?

Ali cut the engine again and jumped out from behind the wheel to circle the car and greet her sister with a hug. "I take it you two have introduced yourselves."

"We're practically old friends by now, right?" Jase asked, eliciting another easy laugh from Helen. He moved to the trunk where he stowed the suitcase—once Ali stopped gaping at the two of them and unlocked it. Helen watched Jase with undisguised interest as Ali watched Helen. She was a married woman. What was she doing watching Jase's every move?

Ali closed her eyes and turned away. She refused to admit to herself that she didn't want another woman interested in him. After all, she had no right to think that.

"I'll sit in the rumble seat," he volunteered, stepping past Helen and sliding into the backseat.

"So you brought him to meet me?" Helen asked Ali with a smile of accomplishment that Ali couldn't miss.

"I must confess. Ali's taking me home," Jase quickly explained, holding up his hand to halt her assumption. "We just took the long detour by the airport and there you were."

"She's taking you home with her?"

Helen looked so hopeful now that Ali gave her arm a playful swat.

"Helen," she said in a low tone.

"Practically," Jase quickly went on to say. "But it's not like I'm a lost puppy who needs a home. We're close neighbors. Isn't that right, Ali? Or didn't you tell Helen about me?"

Ali tried to shut him up with a direct glare and a raised eyebrow as she started the car. Undeterred, he smiled as she drove out toward the entrance ramp to the interstate highway.

"You're her new next-door neighbor, right?" Helen responded enthusiastically. She turned to Ali. "He is the one you told me about."

When Jase nodded and added, "The one and only," Helen clapped her hands and turned a little in her seat to face him.

"Ali is a great neighbor to have close by." Jase folded his arms and leaned them on the back of the front seat as if to share a confidence. "You wouldn't believe all she's done for me. She arranged for dozens of people to phone me with ah . . . unique greetings. She doused me with muddy rainwater, soaking me to the skin, and then offered to do my laundry. After that she took my breakfast rolls away from me."

Ali couldn't resist joining in. "Hey, you offered. And besides, I let you eat one of them," she countered in the same light mood.

"So you did, Ali. And she went out to dinner with me too, Helen. And I just had to pay for my own meal, not hers. She let me pay the next time though."

Ali frowned, wondering why he had brought that up.

"My sister's all heart," Helen offered with a grin.

Jase shook his head. "I don't know. After dinner that first time, she sent me straight home. Wouldn't even offer a cup of coffee to a thirsty man." He sniffled dramatically and sighed.

Ali laughed at how Jase was able to twist the truth to make it sound like something entirely different. He was very good at it.

"You should have heard her today on the way to the airport," Jase continued. "She lectured me on how to behave when you're around. Can you believe it?"

He held up his hand to shield the side of his mouth. "I think she's afraid I'll embarrass her in front of you," he said in a stage whisper that Ali could hear easily. "Just used and tossed aside."

He sighed even more dramatically to make his outrageous point, raising the back of his hand to his forehead. "What a man has to put up with these days!"

Ali shook her head and tried valiantly to stifle her laughter. "Jase! Enough already."

But he and Helen were ignoring her. She decided to concentrate on her driving and let them have their fun even though it was at her expense.

"Jase, you poor thing," Helen said, playing along with his humor and patting his hand in a consoling manner.

As she changed lanes, Ali caught sight of his smile in the rearview mirror. Was he this friendly with all women? Though she'd noticed that he hadn't acted this way toward the women in the movie theater, it was no wonder so many women played chauffeur for him so willingly.

Frowning, she realized the thought angered her and she couldn't figure out why. When she suddenly recognized that she might just be jealous, she straightened in her seat. She had no right to be jealous of other women in Jase's life. Why couldn't she seem to remember that?

"I'm a bit in the dark here," Helen said. "I'd like to hear what you did that made her throw muddy water at you," she explained. "Tell me all. I can't wait to hear. Ali hasn't told me anything about that."

"Helen!" Ali whined.

"Nothing, Helen, I swear," Jase said, still ignoring Ali. He raised his right arm as if he were taking an oath. "I was just standing there, literally minding my own business, when she fired the muddy water at me. I'm completely innocent . . . this time." He sat up straight and winked at Ali in the mirror.

Ali gasped. "Jase!"

Helen appeared to enjoy the show in the backseat and her laughter egged Jase on. "Has Ali invited you to join us for brunch? I'd hoped to get to know some of her friends while I'm here."

"No, and isn't that something? I slave all night to bake the sweet rolls she bought, but does she invite me over to eat some myself? Noooo."

Ali opened her mouth, but she didn't get a chance to get a word in. Helen was too quick.

"Oh, you poor baby. But tell me, Jase. If Ali is already throwing muddy water at you, then you must be important to her. Isn't that a gesture of great significance nowadays?"

"Oh. Do you think so?" Jase asked with faked wide-eyed innocence.

"In your dreams, Jase. In your dreams," Ali muttered loud enough for them both to hear. They laughed more.

"What is she taking you home from, Jase? Were you playing tennis?"

There it was again, his deep, warm laugh. Ali loved that sound and the way it rumbled in his broad chest.

"No, I played at being a baker last night. That's why I'm in the whites. Your breakfast here is from the Dutch Treats shop that I . . . where I was . . . when Ali picked me up after working there all night."

"Picked you up?" Ali squeezed Helen's arm. "Don't listen to him. He has a way of, shall we say, stretching the truth. You know I don't pick up strange men."

"So now I'm a strange man, huh?" Jase laughed with a fake shocked look on his face. "I don't think I'm so strange."

Helen laughed. "Ali, I'll have a chance to get better acquainted with Jase, won't I?"

"Ah . . . sure . . . fine," Ali reassured her sister with a new stammer. "I don't know how long you'll be here, but maybe he can entertain us again at dinner one night before you leave." They'd arrived at their street before any definite plans could be made.

"I hope we can get together soon," Helen said as the car stopped in the driveway.

Ali jumped out from behind the wheel to save Helen the trouble of letting Jase out her side of the two-door car. She stood with her back to the door and held the seat forward as Jase unfolded from the backseat. With his arms extended high in the air, he stretched and his left hand came down to rest on the side of Ali's waist. It felt warm and she was dismayed to realize she liked it there.

With his other arm leaning on the top of the car, he grinned at Helen. "Nice meeting you, Helen. I promise we'll see each other more than just this once. Enjoy your breakfast."

Ali inhaled the sweet smell of the bakery spices that wafted around Jase. Cinnamon. She loved the delicious scent. She associated it with sweet memories of baking Christmas cookies and warm toast at special family breakfasts.

"Thanks, Jase. Hope to see you soon." Helen closed her car door.

When Jase turned back to Ali, she silently hoped he'd merely thank her for the ride, or just say goodbye and go home. Right now she was feeling more of an attraction to him than she thought was wise. She needed to put more distance between them. "Sweet dreams, Jase," she said softly. "Sleep well."

"Thanks for the ride, neighbor."

With no more warning than a gentle squeeze at her waist, he leaned down and kissed her gently on her lips. She felt the kiss to her tippy-toes in a flutter, as if dozens of butterflies had been released inside her. She was startled into silence. The silence lasted until she'd watched him disappear into his house.

"Well, I'll be," Helen said, the grin obvious in her voice. Ali's butterflies disappeared.

"Come on. I'll get your bag." Feeling heat rising into her cheeks, she pulled Helen's suitcase from the trunk and led the way into her house.

"A kiss from a great-looking hunk you told me was just a neighbor? I think you've been holding out on me, little sister. Come on, tell all. Who is that good-looking Dutch confection?" Helen asked as Ali showed her to the guest room.

Ali shrugged. "He told you. He's a baker and a new neighbor."

Helen smiled kindly. "You know, Ali, it's about time there was a man in your life. And to think I worried about you being lonely here in this house."

"Helen!" Ali warned firmly.

"Okay, okay. Even if a romance never develops, it's comforting for me to know there's a nice honest man next door."

"Please. Don't get me started on my lecture about how a woman doesn't need a man to make her 'complete,' or on what I think of your ongoing plans to get me married. Listen, you two had your fun in the car, but Jase is really only a new friend. A neighbor."

"One with a delightful sense of humor."

Ali tapped the plate of fresh bakery goodies. "Yes, and he's an artist. These are his works of art. Wait until you taste them, but I'll warn you. You'll never be happy with eating packaged sweet rolls again. Let me tell you, he works in the best bakery around."

"Good looking, an artist, sense of humor, enjoys being with you, even staked a claim of sorts by kissing you in front of . . ."

"I meant it. Don't even think it, sister dear," Ali warned again. "Jase is just my next-door neighbor, so don't start buying any bridal magazines. Real relationships take time to build, and right now I'm too busy trying to build a business so I can keep up my house payments." Ali opened a box of herbal tea bags.

"Well, just remember how the saying goes: you don't have to look further than your own backyard, or maybe the next-door backyard, to find what you're looking for, Ali."

Ali groaned loudly and poured hot water over the tea bags she'd hung in the pot. "You don't give up, do you? Enough about me. What about you?"

Helen sighed. "Same old, same old. Eric is halfway around the world. I was lonely sitting home all by myself, so I hopped on a plane to come see you. But don't worry. Visiting you doesn't mean you have to spend all your time with me, Ali. I know you're busy. Honest."

"I've got to get my current project done on schedule because I can't postpone the promotion date."

"That's fine. I just needed to get away. The condo seems so empty when Eric is out of town for weeks on end. Besides, you've got to eat meals, and I can talk to you then. The rest of the time I'll vegetate, or I can help you if there's anything I can do."

"Well, let's see," Ali said slowly while trying to look pensive. "You can weed the flower beds. The kitchen floor needs waxing, oh, and I want to replace the non-skid decals on the bottom of the bathtub. That is, of course, if it will help you relax," Ali added facetiously.

"Sounds wonderful," Helen said, laughing hard.

"And when you get bored with all that, I have hundreds of plastic water bottles that need a flexible straw put in and a lid screwed on, and then a bag of promotion goodies tied on each one. That crazy job could drive us both nuts just as easily as it could flip me out doing it alone."

Ali grinned and patted Helen's hand where it rested on the table. "Well, you asked me."

"Sounds like you could use some help, but I think I'll pass on the bathtub decals." The sisters laughed.

"I'm glad you came—whatever the reason."

"Sitting in your backyard sounds wonderful for a change instead of pacing a hole in our living room carpet. And I will help with the promotion you're working on," Helen said.

After they had enjoyed their tea and the dishes were

done, Helen headed for the deck with a book while Ali filled her mug with the last of the tea to take with her to her office. The basket on the shelf containing a few of the newly labeled little bags filled with the remainder of the candy caught her eye. A smile curled up the corners of her lips. She emptied the candy from one bag into another full one and grabbed a rubber band. Folding down the top of the doubly full bag, she walked through the house and slipped out her kitchen door.

Across the driveway, she opened Jase's screen door, being careful not to make any noise that might wake him. She looped the band around the bag and then around the doorknob. Her wee gift would be a sweet addition to her verbal apology for the phone number mix-up. She eased the screen door closed and crossed quickly back to her own house.

She'd apologized and now she'd given him a token gift to reiterate that she was sorry. The end. She no longer had a reason to see him again except to wave in passing as neighbors often did.

No reason at all.

Unless he wanted to call and thank her for the candy. And, of course, she had promised Helen a dinner with him.

Ali stopped with her hand on her doorknob. What was she thinking? Could she forget her anger at Jeff and consider the possibility that Jase could be more than just a friendly and funny neighbor? Her pulse sped up at the thought.

The phone rang as she slipped back into the kitchen. "I'll get it," she called to Helen.

"This is the marketing department secretary for Dutch Treats Bakeries," said a pleasant-voiced woman. "We've received your bid for the promotion coming up when our new bakery opens."

"Yes," Ali said. "I sent that in several weeks ago." *So long ago that I figured I didn't win the bid*, she added to herself.

"Right. I'm calling on behalf of Frank Wilson, the marketing director. He's given your proposal a favorable review, and he'd like you to come in to discuss it further with him."

"I'd be happy to," Ali said, trying to keep the excitement she felt out of her voice. "Should I come to your offices in Syracuse?"

"Actually, I know this is terribly short notice, but he's going to be at the bakery near your company's address this afternoon. If you could see him there, you could go over what you have planned and show him where everything will actually appear. If not, that's fine. Then he would see you here in his offices."

"No, this afternoon is fine." Ali looked at her watch. It was almost afternoon already.

"He left here a few minutes ago, and he'll be there for the better part of the afternoon. What about in an hour? Would that be possible?"

Ali told her it would be fine, thanked her, and ended the call. She headed directly toward the deck to tell Helen but discovered her asleep on the chaise in the shade of the huge maple. Without disturbing her, Ali silently slipped back into the house. She changed out of her jeans into casual business clothes and gathered her materials. She wrote Helen a note to tell her where she would be. Leaning it against the napkin holder on the kitchen table, she headed for the bakery.

An hour and forty-five minutes later, she was home again with an enormous smile on her face. Helen met her in the kitchen as she entered. "Helen, I'm so excited. The interview went tremendously well. I think he was impressed that I'd actually shopped enough in the bakery to know all about it. The marketing manager, Frank Wilson, said he would let me know the final decision on who would handle the promotion as soon as possible." She splayed her hands on her chest and inhaled a deep breath.

"Then they're considering other people for the job?" Helen asked.

"Yeah. He's talking to two others too," Ali said much less enthusiastically. "But that's normal. At least I'm a finalist for the job," she added brightly. Lowering her voice, she added, "Now all I have to do is wait some more. That's the hardest part."

"Won't Jase be surprised when you tell him you might be getting the promotion job at the bakery where he works?"

"Jase?"

"Haven't you told him already, Ali?"

"No. I sent in my bid weeks ago, and since then I've been busy with the candy store promotion and now the one at the new convenience store." She shrugged, palms up. "I haven't thought to mention it since I learned he worked there." She smiled. "But I can't see any reason not to tell him." Her smile was quickly replaced by a frown. "Although, I wouldn't want him to feel he had to put in a good word for me."

"He might not think of doing that." Helen shrugged. "A baker wouldn't have anything to do with the promotions company they hired."

"No," Ali agreed hesitantly.

"So tell him. Jase should get a big kick out of hearing about it."

By late that afternoon Jase had given up all hope of getting any sleep. Trading night for day in his sleep cycle was hard to do in a family neighborhood. All the sounds people took for granted drove him up the wall. Even the innocent, repetitive scrapes of a rake on a nearby lawn had him ready to tear his hair out when he was trying to sleep.

The fact that he couldn't get his mind off Ali also had a good deal to do with his inability to sleep. Meeting her had triggered so many new and unexpected feelings. And what's more, he knew from the look in her eyes that she'd felt the attraction between them.

He'd never dreamed of meeting someone like her right next door. There was no doubt about it, having her for a neighbor could be fun: a nice diversion from the long hours of hard work he put in regularly.

And it was great that she knew nothing about his owning the bakeries. He liked being with a woman who had no ulterior motive for seeing him. She couldn't be after him because of his position or money because she knew nothing about them. He couldn't believe his luck, and he sure wasn't going to blow it now by letting her find out who he was.

Jase punched his pillow and tried again to get comfortable enough to fall back to sleep. Suddenly, he sat up as an idea struck him from out of nowhere.

What if Ali applied for the promotions job at the bakery?

That would blow everything. If she got the job, she'd find out that he owned the company, and that wasn't the way he wanted to tell her. Then she'd think he gave the job to her, whether she deserved it or not, just because they were dating. If she didn't get it, she'd think he was to blame for that too. He couldn't win.

He groaned. Why had he ever thought keeping his identity secret was a good idea?

Grabbing the phone, he punched in the Dutch Treats main office number. He discovered that his marketing director was at the local shop. He called that number.

Frank must have been sitting at the manager's desk because he answered the phone and recognized Jase's voice at once. "I was just going to call you, Jase. I've just interviewed someone for the promotions job. I want to . . ."

Jase cut him off. "That's what I'm calling about, Frank. I don't want to hear about what happened. I want you to make the decision of which company to use without me."

"Without you? What do you mean?"

"Just exactly what I said. I want nothing to do with the selection of the one you hire. Okay?"

"Nothing at all?"

"No. Listen, I've decided to let you handle the bids without my input. That's all. Of course, when you have the meetings with the promoters after you've awarded the contract, I want to come to meet him or her, but I don't want any part of making the decision before that point."

"Do you want to tell me why?" Frank asked after a few moments. "You always try to have a finger in every pot."

Jase laughed. "Yeah. I guess I do. Let's just say I've decided to stay in the shadows for this one. You've worked for me almost from day one. I'm not worried about your decisions."

"You're the boss," Frank said. "And if that's the way you want to handle this, then I guess I don't have anything more to report at this point."

"Thanks, Frank. See you back at the office tomorrow."

Smiling, Jase hung up and rolled over on his back. The afternoon sun shone in around the room-darkening windowshades and the navy-colored drapes. The direct sunlight was the last straw. He swung his long legs out of the bed and got up.

When he was dressed, he crossed to his desk and dialed Ali's phone number.

Chapter Six

"That spaghetti sauce smells delicious! And you made your wonderful little meatballs," Ali exclaimed as she entered the kitchen following a refreshing bubble bath to relax her after working all afternoon.

"My turn to cook and I remembered you liked my recipe."

"I love it. Say, did I hear the phone ringing while I was soaking?"

"Yup. It was Jase," Helen answered matter-of-factly as she continued cutting up fresh vegetables for a salad.

Ali tried for the same casual tone. "The Jase next door?"

Helen looked at Ali over her shoulder. "You know more than one?" Helen asked with a silly smile on her face that made Ali suspicious.

Ali shook her head. "What did Jase want?" she asked cautiously.

"He made me an offer I couldn't refuse." Ali's double take made Helen laugh. "He asked me if I wanted to trade him a dinner for fresh French bread and dessert."

"Let me guess. Um . . ." Her index finger tapping her chin, Ali looked up a few moments. "Hmmm." She looked at Helen and pointed her index finger at her. "I know. You told him you'd hold out for a better offer."

Helen laughed. "Gosh, I never thought of that. Maybe I could have gotten rolls for breakfast too. But I don't want to get the man into trouble for taking too many baked goods home from the store."

Helen dropped a handful of shaved carrots into the bowl of greens. "I got to choose the dessert though. We're having cream puffs filled with chocolate mousse, sprinkled with powdered sugar, and drizzled with chocolate glaze." Ali groaned. "I couldn't resist. Doesn't that sound heavenly? Of course, we won't talk about the calories."

"Considering the deep and unconditional love for chocolate that we share, I'd say the dessert sounds perfect. But since when don't you complain about calories? You're really a different woman since the last time I saw you, Helen. Are you sure there's not an alien in your body who's taking control over you?"

For just a split second, Ali saw a look of surprise cross Helen's face. The look disappeared almost as quickly as Helen laughed.

"One time won't hurt and I thought we needed a treat." She sighed dramatically. "And Jase is so good-looking that I thought eating dinner across the table from him would be fun," she said dreamily. Then she straightened and spoke in a warning tone. "Of course, if you tell Eric I said that, I'll deny it," she joked and sighed loudly again for effect. "To think you live next door to him."

"Will you cut it out? This isn't a real big suburb, Helen. He has to live somewhere."

"Yeah, but he's handsome, has a good sense of humor. He's patient and kind."

"Okay, okay, Helen, and I'm sure he doesn't kick dogs or yell at children either, but put away your matchmaker hat."

"Why? I think you deserve a nice guy like Jase."

"Oh, come on. It took days before we could even get together for dinner. We both work crazy hours. Our schedules aren't compatible for dating, plus I don't think I'm in his league. I think he moves too fast and with too many women at once."

A taxi pulling into the driveway announced Jase's arrival and stopped the sisters' conversation. Ali found herself wishing Jase's car would be fixed soon. Taxis in this town were expensive and she hated that he had to pay for rides.

With a friendly greeting, he strolled in the kitchen door dressed in navy cotton slacks and a navy and white knit shirt. He handed Helen a long loaf of bread and a box of desserts.

"Oh, Ali, will you look at these? They're works of art," Helen declared when she opened the box.

"Really? Art? Hmmm. Maybe we should raise prices," Jase responded. The trio laughed. "What can I do to help?"

Ali had sliced the French bread by the time Helen and Jase had carried the remainder of the dinner things out to the table on the deck.

"I've never been able to get French bread crusty like this. Or as delicious," Helen said as they ate.

"You mean you've tried to make French bread at home?" Jase asked. "You're fearless in the kitchen."

"Well, I don't work outside the home, so I have the time. I like puttering around in the kitchen."

"I can vouch for some fun times in your kitchen," Ali remarked. "Remember the first time you tried to make rye bread and I was there to help?"

"I still laugh each time I think of it," Helen said with a grin.

"What happened?" Jase asked.

"We made doorstops instead of bread, that's what happened," Ali told him. "The loaves were flat and heavy." She laughed at the memory. "We kept baking them longer and longer, thinking they still had to rise more."

Helen laughed as she listened. "And when we finally gave up on them getting any bigger and took them out of the oven, one slipped off the pan and almost broke a tile on the floor, it was so hard." She wiped away a tear.

"Be glad your foot wasn't under it," Jase told her.

Helen erupted in brief laughter again but then asked, "Tell us, what did we do wrong?"

"Probably killed the yeast," he answered. "The dough couldn't rise, so it was heavy and dense."

"It sure was," Helen agreed. "We ended up putting it on the apartment windowsill for the birds . . ."

"And they didn't even want it," Ali finished with another laugh. "We had to smash the loaves with a hammer to break them up into pieces before the birds would touch it."

"You ever have a failure like ours?" Helen asked Jase.

"Have I ever," he admitted. He entertained them with tales of recipes gone bad and recipes that never made it to the store shelves.

After they finished eating, the trek back to the kitchen with the food and dishes was quickly accomplished by all three.

"That dinner was delicious. I'm glad I invited myself over," Jase told the sisters.

"Good food and fun too," Ali said.

Helen paused on the deck and looked west. "A spectacular dinner show, too. I can't see a sunset like that over the building next to ours in Chicago."

"I don't think I've ever seen such a beautiful fuchsia, gold, and purple layered sunset, and it's perfectly framed between those giant maples at the corners of the yard," Jase noted.

"What did I tell you? The man thinks like an artist too," Helen said.

"Well, that's the last of the dishes, done nicely by our six-handed effort, thank you," Ali said quickly. "I've got an idea. Let's all go for a walk to work off the yummy cream puffs before it gets completely dark out."

"It's a beautiful evening for it," Helen agreed. "But I'm going to stretch out and read the next chapter in the book I started. You two go on without me."

"Helen," Ali warned. She felt annoyed that Helen was bowing out and peeved at her continued efforts to get her alone with Jase.

He didn't seem to notice, however. "The evening is perfect for walking." He took Ali's hand before she could object and led the way back out onto the deck. "Come on. I'll walk with you." He slid the door closed behind them.

"Wait. Just look at the finale of that sunset," Ali said. "It's gorgeous. I'm continually amazed at nature's beauty."

Leaning closer, Jase turned Ali's face to his with just a finger under her chin. "Me too." He lowered his head until their lips touched. His kiss was warm and gentle.

Ali knew she should move away but she couldn't get her legs to go along with the idea. When Jase lifted his head, their gazes locked. Ali raised her fingers to touch his cheek. "I thought we agreed that this wouldn't be a good idea," she whispered.

Jase stepped a little closer and wrapped his strong arms around her waist. Ali's hands moved of their own volition to his shoulders. They kissed again so sweetly that Ali couldn't imagine why she'd thought it was a bad idea.

When Helen walked right past the sliding door to the deck on her way to the kitchen, the kiss ended abruptly, but Jase didn't step back.

"You guys resting already after the ten long steps it took to get that far?" Helen called out with a chuckle.

Ali felt like a teenager caught necking on the couch by her mother. She dropped her forehead to Jase's shoulder, but neither of them moved apart. She felt him shake with silent laughter.

The refrigerator door opened and shut, and they watched Helen wave as she passed by the door again on her way to the living room, a bottle of water in her hand.

"I think we've rested up enough now to continue our walk," Jase called after her.

He reluctantly took hold of Ali's wrist and led her around the house toward the driveway. "Come on for that walk, Ali. The fireflies will light our way."

Ali was working very late again. Helen had gone to bed at a normal hour and Ali had returned to her desk to finish in order to free up daylight time to spend touring the area with her sister.

She jumped when the phone rang. Her first thought was that middle-of-the-night calls always meant terrible news, like the call she'd gotten about her parents' deaths. Could it be about Eric? She grabbed the receiver on the first ring.

"I was wondering, when's your birthday?"

Ali let out the breath she'd been holding. "Jase? You called me at two in the morning to ask me when my birthday is?"

"I just came home and noticed your light was on, so I thought I'd call."

Ali laughed. "Sure you did, Jase. How far out into your backyard did you have to walk to be able to see the light in my office?"

"Caught me, huh?"

There was that warm, deep chuckle of his again.

"So when is your birthday, Ali?"

"May twenty-third."

"Mmm. I bet you were a beautiful baby."

"I was chubby," she answered, but she wasn't sure she wanted him to know that. "Jase, what do you want? Why'd you call? I still have more work to do."

"Just wanted to say hi."

"But you're home and it's the middle of the night. Why aren't you asleep already? You never seem to have enough time off to catch up."

"Actually, I can catch up on weekends because I don't work in the bakery overnight then. Well, practically never. A woman who moonlights from her day job works weekend nights. She's generally reliable and very capable, a dear named Emma. Her specialties are coffee cakes and Danishes, which are perfect for the Saturday and Sunday morning breakfast shoppers. She seems to enjoy doing all the individual time-taking motions necessary for creating those. I can relax weekends in the fresh air and have a good time once in a while."

"You work terribly long hours, Jase. Couldn't you ask your boss to give you more reasonable hours? Switching your sleep cycle so often can't be good for your health."

"Why, Ali, it warms my heart that you care enough to worry about me. But you're a fine one to talk about working long hours when you're still up at this hour of the night too."

"Hey, wait a minute. Didn't you leave for work hours ago? What are you doing home in the middle of the night walking around in your backyard to see my light on? Oh, no. You weren't fired, were you?"

"No, don't worry." Jase chuckled. "They couldn't do that. I just came home to get the recipe I left for a new cookie I've been working on. Doesn't a dot of raspberry on a buttery square of shortbread with a few stripes of chocolate on top sound good?"

"Mmm."

"I'll bring you some in the morning if it works."

Ali groaned. "You can bring me some even if they don't work! Raspberries are my all-time favorite fruit.

Put them on something with chocolate and hold it under my nose and I'll follow you anywhere."

"I'll have to remember that," he said with a soft chuckle. "Well, I gotta go. Sweet dreams, Ali."

Ali couldn't seem to get her mind back on the promotion she was planning after Jase left to go back to work. Better to sleep now and start again in the morning, she decided as she trudged down the hall to bed.

Opening her kitchen door the next morning, she found the bag of fresh cookies Jase had left there. The yummy delicacies put a smile on her face that stayed all day.

Ali carried two glasses filled with iced lemonade to the deck and she sat down at the table. Helen joined her and plopped down on the chaise, stretched out her legs, and wiggled her bare toes. "Eric should see you now," Ali kidded. "Barefoot and sitting in the sun."

But one look at her sister's face told Ali that what she'd said was anything but funny. Helen's eyes were suddenly ringed with red and tears glistened beneath her lowered lashes. Ali leaned over to cover her sister's hand with her own.

"What is it? I've upset you. I'm so sorry. What did I say?"

Helen shook her head and sniffled back her tears. "Oh, Ali. I . . . I miss Eric. I need to talk to him, but I can't. He's been so far away and for so long."

Ali moved to sit on the chaise beside Helen's legs and took her hand. "But he'll be back before you know it. When he gets home, you could take a mini-vacation with him. A second honeymoon. You'll have plenty of time to talk then."

"Oh, sure. A vacation? I'll believe it when I see it happening. Every time we plan a trip for the two of us, something always comes up. He ends up flying off and leaving me alone."

Ali handed Helen a tissue. "I guess it can't be easy having a husband who is a troubleshooter for a major oil company. He's gone a lot, huh?"

"Seems like he's gone all the time. I sort of got used to it after a while, but there are times when I need him badly, like now, and he's not there."

Helen wiped her nose. "I called his office. They said he was due back in the States this week. I told his secretary where I was and left them your number."

"Good. He'll be back sooner than you think."

"I wish I could believe that," she sobbed.

Ali leaned over to hug her. When Helen's tears were spent, Ali proposed a plan to take her sister's mind off her problems.

"How would you like to drive to a lake and stick your feet in the water to cool off? We could go feed the ducks."

Helen smiled, but her lip quivered. "Thanks, but no. Let's stay here. Maybe Eric will call me later this afternoon."

"Sure. He'll call, Helen. I know he will."

Ali hated to see her sister hurting, but that's what her workaholic husband was doing to her. Husbands who worked all the time, all hours of the day and night, left their wives alone and made them worry.

She would be wise to remember that.

Ali closed the kitchen door and headed for the garage to get her car. With an extra mouth to feed this week, she needed to make another quick trip to the grocery store. She was making a mental list of what to buy and paused as she dug her keys from her purse.

Without making a sound, Jase sneaked up behind her and surprised her with a soft kiss on the side of her neck. Not realizing he was even there, Ali jumped a mile. Her rising shoulder blade came into sharp contact with his face.

"Ugh!" he grunted as his head jerked up.

Ali spun around to face him, immediately contrite. He pressed his bruised lower lip against the back of his wrist and then looked at his hand to see if it was bleeding.

"Oh, Jase. I'm sorry." She held his face in her hands and ran her thumb across his lower lip. She was relieved to see that his mouth wasn't swelling. "I'm not in the habit of having men come up behind me and kiss me. Does your lip hurt? It doesn't look like it's swelling, but I could get you some ice."

He shook his head and she could see his Adam's apple bob when he swallowed. "Just so it doesn't bleed on my clothes." Ali realized then that he was dressed in a sharp charcoal gray suit and tie. "I just came in from picking a few strawberries," he said, holding up hands full with plump red berries.

"You're the best-dressed strawberry picker I've ever seen," Ali said.

"I thought I'd set a new tone for the neighborhood." Jase spun around like a model before a camera. "Think summer-weight wool will catch on in the garden?" Ali laughed and shook her head. "Hey. Can you come in for something cool to drink?"

"I guess so. I'm not on a deadline other than to arrive back at home with some groceries by mealtime."

"Whew!" Jase said with exaggerated relief. "If you said no, I didn't know how I was going to open the door for myself with my hands full of berries."

Ali stepped ahead of him and dutifully opened his kitchen door. He laid the plump strawberries beside the sink and rinsed off his hands.

"You look very handsome all dressed up," Ali noted as she closed the door.

"Thanks, but I wear a suit only when I have to. I think it's crazy that people believe that brain power or business acumen is related to what a guy wears." His hands dry, he turned back to her. "On the other hand, if you think I look really good in a suit, I might wear it more often."

"You're fishing, Mr. VanDam. And if you think I'm

going to tell you that I think you look great in whatever you wear, even though you do, you've got another think coming."

"I think you just did." His grin was contagious.

"You know, you're full of surprises, Jase."

"I am?"

"Yeah. You work as a baker, but when you work in daylight hours, you always dress like . . . I don't know. Like you owned the place." Ali laughed at the idea and shook her head.

"Well, you know what they say about dressing for success," Jase said somewhat uneasily after a moment.

Ali felt embarrassed for having suggested that his job as a baker didn't warrant his looking nice during the day.

"Well, I'll go change."

"Can I fix the beverages?"

"If you would like to while I get out of this straight jacket, there's a pitcher of iced tea in the fridge. Cubes are in the ice maker in the freezer."

Ali was carrying the frosty glasses into the living room when Jase returned from changing. "Lots of ice means not so much tea, I found out. But I had so much fun playing with your ice dispenser," she joked.

He came to stand close to her and took one of the glasses. "Thanks." He took a sip. "Hey. Wanna neck on the couch?" he teased with a dramatically lecherous gleam in his eye and wiggling eyebrows.

Groaning at his Groucho impersonation, she shook her head. Stepping around him, she sat on the couch, dropped off her sandals, and folded her legs under her. "Jase?"

He looked down at her. She had his total attention.

Chapter Seven

"**J**ase, would I embarrass myself if I told you I find myself praying a lot when I'm with you?" Ali asked with a grin she couldn't stifle.

He gave her a puzzled look. "I beg your pardon?" He dropped down on the couch several inches away from her.

"I do. Honest. And most of the prayers begin with 'Lead me not into temptation!'"

Jase nodded and chuckled. "Now I see what you mean." Leaning his elbow on the back of the couch, he toyed with the side of Ali's hair, winding it around his finger. As short as it was, it popped free and he tried again.

Instead of leaning against his hand as she wanted to, she sipped her iced tea. Suddenly, it wasn't difficult for her to drink the tea down in short order. The ice clinked in her empty glass. "Thanks for the tea, Jase."

She looked up to meet his gaze and he rubbed her cheek with the back of his knuckles. "I've got to get going," she said. "Helen must be really hungry by now."

Rising quickly, she walked to the counter by the sink and set down her glass. A few seconds later, Jase's half-full glass appeared next to it. He reached for her shoulders and turned her to face him directly.

Ali sighed and smiled. "Jase. You need to get a government license."

"What on earth for?" he asked with a frown.

"I shouldn't admit it, but you touch me and I forget what I was doing. You could get a job as some evil country's secret weapon because you can disable women so fast."

He chuckled. "Not women . . . woman. You, Ali. Only you. And disabling you wasn't what I had in mind at all."

Ali laughed. "Jase, that's what I'm afraid of. We've got to do something about this."

"Good idea," he answered as he lowered his lips to cover hers.

When he'd lifted his head and Ali could speak, it was little more than a hesitant whisper. "Jase, that's not what I had in mind by doing something. I want to go home now."

"No, you don't," he contradicted softly with a smile.

"Well, maybe on some level you're right. It may not be what I want to do, but it's what I will do."

He smiled. "That I can believe ... and it's okay then, Ali."

"Here I go again admitting what I shouldn't, but that's one of the reasons I like you."

"You like me?"

She laughed. "I certainly wouldn't have let you kiss me if I didn't like you, Jase."

"That's good." He kissed her on the nose and walked with her to the door. "Ali, I like being with you and I want to spend more time with you."

"But you're dangerous for me to be around." His head jerked in her direction. "Oh, I enjoy being with you, all right. But I want us to be friends. I can't ... get so involved."

"Thank you, I think. But I can do friends, and hey, friends go out together. Tell you what, let me take you and Helen to dinner tomorrow night. Anywhere you want to go." His face twisted in a grimace. "But do you think you could drive again?"

Ali raised her hands to her hips. "When is your car going to be fixed?"

He shrugged. "They keep saying any day now."

She shook her head. "They could rebuild a car by now."

"That's about what they're doing. When I found the car, it was in really bad shape. It needed body work and a new engine."

"Wouldn't buying another car have been easier? And I would guess cheaper too."

He laughed. "Yeah, but I rarely seem to take the easy way out of anything."

"But the repairs are taking ages. Maybe you should talk to another garage about it."

"This one is okay. The car's so old that they're still having trouble finding some parts, but it's close to being done."

"I can't imagine going to so much trouble for an old car."

"I love old cars." Jase smiled. "And when I get attached to something that's a real keeper, whatever it is, I don't want to let go, ever. If something or somebody is worth it, I'd spend all the time in the world on them."

He ran his bent knuckles down her cheek again. "Ali, I mean it. I want to spend time with you. Say you want it too."

She backed out of his reach and stood closer to the door, her hand on the knob, ready to escape. Her stomach clenched as she tried to stay focused on what she had to say. "Jase, we're neighbors and, I hope, friends. I think that the situation would be difficult, living next door as we do, if we were . . . anything else."

Jase looked surprised at first, then more content. He shrugged. "Maybe you're right. Okay, fine." His hands slapped against his thighs as he moved a step away. "We can be friends."

Could she be wishing he hadn't agreed so easily? "Jase, I . . ."

"No, it's okay." He ran his hand through his hair and

suddenly leaned back against the counter facing her. "But dinner is still on for tomorrow night?"

Ali nodded, realizing she didn't want to cancel it.

"Good. Well, you want to be just friends? I'll show you just friends." He extended his arm, and they shook hands on the arrangement as if it were a business deal.

"So, I'll see you tomorrow night," she proposed with a pleased smile when they had dropped their arms to their sides.

"Right," Jase responded. A little frown creased his forehead as he watched her leave.

As she crossed the driveway to get her car out to finally go to the grocery store, she lectured herself. *I can't forget what Jeff did. I need to be wary and not get to the point of caring for Jase—other than as a friend. That's all I should be interested in, and that way I won't risk another failed relationship. Once was enough. More than enough.*

So she and Jase would just be friends. That's what she wanted. And he'd agreed, so she'd gotten what she asked for, but somehow she felt as if she'd just made a big mistake.

Jase watched Ali cross the driveway to her car. Why had her insistence that they be just friends bothered him so much? Originally, he was interested in a fun time when he was with her, but now it didn't seem like being friends would be the kind of fun he'd had in mind.

More importantly, just having a fun time with Ali no longer interested him. But why had his intent changed?

Because he was thirty maybe? Old enough to think about finding a woman he wanted as his future wife and the mother of his children?

Startled by his own answer, he thought about it a few minutes. If that was the case, he decided, he would like to settle down with a woman like Ali: responsible and intelligent, with a good head on her shoulders. He smiled. She had an adorable head on her shoulders.

It would be great if his future wife had a good sense of humor like Ali's, too. And she was so easy to talk to.

Yeah, Jase thought, if he were to start looking for a wife (though he wasn't ready to admit that he would), she'd have to be a woman who was a whole lot like Ali.

The restaurant Jase directed Ali to faced Lake Oneida.

"Look at all those brightly colored sails. I thought sails were white," Helen remarked. "I can see I don't get out enough," she added with a laugh.

From her seat at the table beside the window, Ali could see the white froth capping the waves in sharp contrast to the deep blue of the cold, clear water. "I knew sails could be colored, but I've never been on a sailboat," Ali said as they all continued to watch the boats. "I wonder what it would be like to speed across the water with only the sound of the wind in the sails."

"I'll take you out in the one I'm going to own some-day," Jase promised lightly.

"As hard and long as you work, Jase, you would

never have time to even get it wet," Ali surmised with a smile, to soften the truth in what she was saying. Jase glanced at her and admitted that she was probably right.

The meal passed all too quickly. The waitress appeared to inquire about more coffee, but all three declined.

After she left to get the check, Ali commented, "It's too bad the new Dutch Treats bakery isn't open. We pass so close to it on the way home that we could have gotten dessert there."

"If it's so close, could we drive by on the way home anyway?" Helen asked. "I'd like to see where it is."

"That would be no trouble if Ali doesn't mind a little detour," Jase remarked. Twenty minutes later they drove into the bakery parking lot.

"This building is sharp, with all those huge windows across the front. A great location, but then I'm sure that's why the company put it here," Ali concluded.

"There's sure plenty of room for parking," Helen remarked as she surveyed the parking lot.

"Yeah, and they're blacktopping it all so there won't be any potholes filled with water after a rainstorm," Jase added, pointedly looking at Ali.

"That will take all the sport out of driving across it," Ali said with a laugh.

Helen rubbed a spot clean on the front window and peered inside.

"I'll show you inside if you want," Jase offered.

"Great, but how come they gave you keys?" Helen had asked the same question that had popped into Ali's head.

"I have the key . . . in case . . ." Jase stammered. "In case they want me to open up in the morning when the crew chief forgets the key," he finally said as he unlocked the door with a ring of keys to rival a school janitor's. "I forgot to leave them after work," he added with a shrug.

As they walked into the partially completed bakery, he immediately began explaining the layout. The keys easily forgotten, Ali found herself walking beside him while Helen followed several feet behind them.

"I like the new showroom here so much more than the other one near home," he explained. "This one surrounds the customer with self-service product shelves. The clerks will only package the small or fragile items, like cookies. Out here it would be too tempting to pop a few right into your mouth instead of the bag."

"It's disappointing not to be able to trust people," Ali responded with a shake of her head. "I've had enough experience to make me an expert. Only it went a lot further than stealing cookies."

"It's tougher when you care for somebody who would deliberately try to deceive you," Helen put in.

"That kind of deception hurts deeply," Ali added, thinking of Jeff and his lies.

"And if the trust between two people is destroyed, so is the relationship. For good," Helen concluded.

Ali nodded and glanced at Jase. He didn't meet her gaze. Saying nothing, he turned away and kicked a small piece of wallboard aside. She wondered why he looked so uncomfortable.

"Sorry, Jase," Ali said. "We didn't mean to get so serious and spoil your tour. Go on with what you were saying about the bakery."

Turning to face her, he stared at her a few moments. Suddenly, he ran his hand through his hair and moved to stare out the window. "I guess that's about all there is to the tour."

Ali glanced at Helen and their gazes locked. Helen frowned and Ali shook her head just a little before she looked back at Jase. Helen shrugged. They both noticed that something was bothering Jase, but neither of them could guess what it was.

"I can almost smell the bread baking," Helen remarked lightly.

Ali felt responsible for darkening the mood of the conversation when they had been having so much fun. "That's my sister. A very imaginative nose," Ali teased to improve the mood.

"Better imaginative than big," Helen retorted, tapping the tip of her nose.

Jase turned to face Helen without a glance toward Ali. "Helen, smelling bread has got to be better than the paint and plaster dust I smell here tonight. But wait until this shop opens. I'll bet the neighbors complain that the bread and spicy fragrances drive them to eating more."

"Will you work in this new bakery?" Helen asked. "Or stay at the bakery near your house?"

He shrugged and raised his hands palms up. "Ah, I've worked for the company since it began and I go where I'm needed . . . where they send me. I'm over here with stuff from the office for the contractors every once in a while." He shrugged and looked less than pleased to be talking about his job again.

Suddenly, Ali sneezed twice in rapid succession. "Pardon me. I don't know what's gotten into me, but I think . . ." She sneezed again.

"Now I think my sister's nose is trying to tell us something," Helen said with a laugh.

"I'm sorry. I can't seem to sto—" Ali didn't get out the rest of the word before she was sneezing again. Looking through her pockets for a tissue yielded nothing.

"Ali, are you allergic to dust?" Jase asked.

"It sort of gets to me when there's a lot of it." Looking in her purse, she promptly sneezed again and then gave up her tissue search.

With a laugh Jase offered her his handkerchief and slipped his arm around her waist to steer her to the door. "End of tour. Time for fresh air for you."

Ali took the clean folded cloth and tried to blow her nose without making too much noise. She stayed tucked against Jase's side all the way outside. In the fresh air, she stopped sneezing. She wiped her nose one last time and pushed his handkerchief into her purse.

"I'll wash and iron it before I return it," she assured him with a grin.

"Do you want me to drive home?" he asked.

"Thanks, but I'm fine now."

In their driveway after an enjoyable drive home, Ali stopped to let Jase and Helen exit the car before pulling into the garage. Her sister asked him if he would like to come in for a while. "I made some cold raspberry tea this afternoon. It's really good with the raspberry dot cookies Ali picked up today."

"Sure. You were at the shop today, Ali?" Jase asked as she followed them into her kitchen once the garage was closed and locked.

"Why do you look surprised? I'm there often, Jase. It's the best bakery in town. That's the third time this week that . . . Oh, Jase! I forgot again to tell you." She grinned broadly.

"Whatever it is, you look excited," he said as Helen got out the tea and handed him the pitcher to set on the counter.

"I never told you I put in a bid for the promotions job at Dutch Treats for when the new one we just saw opens."

Jase almost dropped the tea pitcher. It hit the hard surface of the counter with a clunk. "Sorry. I didn't realize how slippery the glass was." He smiled weakly.

On a roll, Ali explained her promotions ideas while Helen poured the tea. "It shouldn't be hard to have two costumes made to match the Dutch boy and girl on the logo. Their appearances around town would keep the logo in the public's mind."

Strangely quiet, Jase didn't even look at her directly as she spoke. She guessed he must not have liked her ideas, but he was too polite to say anything. She cut short her explanation.

"Well, good, but I don't have anything to do with picking who gets the contract," he said with a shrug.

"Oh, I know that. I just thought you'd be interested in the fact that I applied. You know. Wish me luck and all that."

With a smile that never reached his eyes, he wished her good luck in getting the job and drank his tea quickly. Not much later, after only polite conversation, he excused himself and went home.

Helen yawned. "The evening has been lovely, but I'm going to bed," she announced, putting her glass in the sink.

"Just a minute, Helen. Didn't you think Jase acted strangely tonight?" Ali asked as she popped the dirty glasses into the dishwasher.

"Well, since you asked, I have to admit that I expected him to be more excited about your bid to work at the bakery."

"Me too," Ali agreed. "The conversation seemed to go downhill after I brought it up."

"Well, some guys need their own private territory when they're in a relationship. Maybe he thinks you're moving into his by putting in the bid where he works. Would you be above him in salary or position for the time you're there?"

Ali shrugged. "Maybe, but you're really comparing apples to oranges. No one would compare the two positions that way."

"The difference or similarity may not be significant to you, but it might be to him. Something bothers him. That's for sure."

"I don't know, but I agree with you, Helen. I could see it at the new bakery too. Something seemed to make him very uncomfortable."

"Well, we weren't very gracious when we turned down his offer to buy both our dinners. It was almost a knock-down drag-out fight when we all reached for the bill at the same time."

"I know," Ali hedged. "But he can't be making that much as a baker. And he shouldn't have to pay for our dinners. I hope his male pride didn't suffer, though."

After a quick shower, Jase fell into bed. From that moment Ali explained her promotions ideas, he'd felt his world tilt. But he shouldn't have been surprised. Deep down, he'd known all along that she would apply for the job. Seeing how hard she worked to expand her business, he had to know.

Why had he let himself get into this mess? And why hadn't he been honest with her from the start and told her he owned the stores? The longer he continued the charade of being just a baker, the more he regretted it. He didn't like being dishonest, but he never dreamed it would be such a big deal.

Now what could he do? He'd never considered himself a coward, but suddenly he was. He was afraid that telling her would hurt her. And the last thing he wanted to do was hurt her.

He didn't want to lose her either. And when she found out he'd been lying to her since they'd met, he knew he would lose her. It wasn't that she would hate the idea that he owned the bakeries. She would hate that he had lied to her and destroyed the trust they had been building. She'd said as much during the tour at the new bakery.

Jase lay awake for a long time, trying to figure out what to do. There had to be a way out, a way to tell her that wouldn't destroy her trust. There had to be.

He just couldn't think of it.

Chapter Eight

"There's the mailman," Helen called from the living room just as Ali heard his steps on the porch. The bang of the mail slot sounded against her front door.

Ali picked up the letters from the entry floor and shuffled through them as the phone rang. She grabbed the portable phone; it was Frank Wilson, the promotions manager at Dutch Treats.

"I wanted to congratulate you and tell you that we would like to offer you the contract for the promotions for the new store in the chain of Dutch Treats bakeries."

"I got it!" Ali said to Helen, covering her end of the phone.

"Got what?" Helen whispered as she lowered her book to her lap.

"The promotions contract for Dutch Treats," Ali whispered back.

"I really liked your ideas," Wilson continued, "and I'm looking forward to talking about them more with you so we can get started."

Uncovering the phone, Ali said, "That's great. I'm really looking forward to it too."

"Good. I'd like you to come to a meeting at the corporate headquarters in Syracuse," he replied.

"Of course."

"You'll be meeting the Dutch Treats president, Jason VanDam, who's looking forward to meeting the person handling the promotion."

Ali gasped. Feeling shock and total, cold numbness, she dropped down hard on the arm of Helen's chair. "Oh, no. He wouldn't. Not him too."

"I beg your pardon?" Wilson said.

"What? Oh, I'm sorry, but I'll have to call you back," Ali managed before she ended the call and dropped the phone into the easy chair beside Helen.

She had been betrayed and lied to—again. Her throat closed and she fought to draw in a ragged breath.

"Ali?" Helen whispered. When she got no response, she grasped Ali's arm and shook it gently. "Ali, what is it? You look so pale all of a sudden. Honey, what's wrong?"

Moisture welled in Ali's eyes as she stared straight ahead. In a monotone, she told Helen, "I'm supposed to meet the owner of the whole chain of Dutch Treats bakeries. The marketing guy said he is looking forward to meeting the promotions person handling the grand opening." She took a deep breath. "The owner's name is Jason VanDam."

"No, it couldn't be Jase. He . . . he . . ." Helen stammered.

"Yeah. I couldn't think of a reason it couldn't be him either," Ali said quietly.

"Well, now we know how he could get us into the new bakery with his big ring of keys."

"You know, I was even worried that night that he might get into trouble because he let us see the place." She groaned loudly. "Oh, Helen, he's been lying to me about everything since I met him."

"I'm so sorry, hon. He seems so nice."

"When I think of the times I . . ." Ali raised her fingers to her lips, remembering the kisses they'd shared. She inhaled deeply again and blinked at the stinging tears she was barely managing to keep from falling down her cheeks. "How could he deceive me like that? When I told him about applying for this job with his company, I was so excited and he acted so distracted. What an idiot I was."

She grabbed two handfuls of hair and pulled as she cried out to vent her anger, her hurt, and her deep disappointment. Then she slapped her hands down on her thighs. "I must have a big sign on my back that says, 'Lie to me!' "

She dropped her face into her hands and sniffled. "And just when I think I was falling in love with him."

Helen put her arm on Ali's back and stroked back and forth. "You had no way of knowing, hon."

Ali looked down at Helen. "It never occurred to me to ever ask who the owner was. Maybe I should have found out, but I didn't because all the dealings I had were with the marketing director. I guess I didn't think I'd ever meet the owner unless he showed up at the opening event."

"What are you going to do?"

Wiping her tears on the backs of her hands, Ali rose and began pacing back and forth in front of Helen's chair. "I don't know. I'm not over feeling angry and hurt yet." She stopped and faced Helen. "Why didn't he tell me?"

"Who can tell? But I do know you shouldn't be angry at yourself," Helen assured her.

"But how could I be so gullible? And why didn't I guess who he was? Now that I know he's the owner, the signs are so obvious."

"Hindsight is always better."

"But I should have known something didn't fit right. Am I just a lousy judge of men?"

"No, hon, it's simple. You wanted to believe him. You wanted to trust him because you cared for him."

Ali looked out the window without seeing anything in particular. "Yeah, you're right," she said softly, but then turned away. "But now I can't believe that he wanted to spend time with me for any reason—other than for another notch on his bedpost," she said, getting angry all over again.

"You can't let yourself get worked up." Helen rose and reached out her hand toward Ali.

"Oh no? Just watch me."

"Ali, what are you going to do?" Helen asked with a frown.

Ali tried to smile. She didn't want to upset Helen. "Don't worry. I'm not going to do something rash. I'm okay. Really. I'm going to call the manager back with my apologies for practically hanging up on him and arrange the appointment he wanted to make with me," she said. "I may be a lousy judge of a man's integrity level, but I'm not a coward."

She sniffled and strode to the hallway. Then she stopped and turned back to Helen. "In fact, I'm going to the Dutch Treats main office as soon as I can. I'm going to tell Mr. Jason VanDam in person just what I think of his deceit."

Ali walked down the hall into her office and dialed Frank Wilson's phone number. Sounding happy to hear from her so soon after the abrupt end to his call, he happily said he would look forward to seeing her first thing the following morning.

Ali dressed carefully for her appointment at Dutch Treats. She chose her navy "power" suit that always gave her confidence. She'd lain awake late into the night trying to figure out why Jase had lied to her, but she came up with no answers other than that he was having fun at her expense.

She would end her relationship with him and that would be the end of the promotion job too. She hated losing the contract, which would be a big boost for her business, but she couldn't take it now. Her excitement and pleasure had been so intense when she learned that she'd gotten the job. Until she heard the name of the company's president, she never doubted that she'd earned the job because of her ability, drive, and experience.

But when she heard Jase's name, it all came tumbling down. It didn't matter how good she was at promotions. She would always wonder: would she have gotten the job if she hadn't known him?

But so what? She would show him that she could do okay without him. Her business was expanding and would continue to expand without the Dutch Treats job.

And she would get along nicely without a relationship with him too. She'd thrived after losing Jeff and she wouldn't pack it in now either. She would continue to wait until she found her Mr. Right. Somewhere, there had to be a man for her as bright and witty as Jase. She chewed on her lower lip. There was probably no chance that he would be as good-looking as Jase. But that didn't matter. She refused to believe that her Mr. Right didn't exist. Her only worry was that Mr. Right would have a tough act to follow in Jase.

Ali left early for her appointment and had to drive

through the morning rush-hour traffic heading into Syracuse. But she wanted to arrive on time and found the Dutch Treats headquarters with no problem. As she entered the area, she just headed for the huge picture on the side of the brick building of the costumed Dutch boy and girl in wooden shoes, holding a partially sliced loaf of bread between them on a Delft plate.

Ali recognized the secretary who greeted her as being the one who drove Jase home on several occasions. She couldn't forget the long auburn hair that flowed over her shoulders. Dressed in a gored skirt with a silk blouse and sweater, she seemed friendly and capable.

Unwillingly, Ali found herself imagining what the secretary did all day: working closely with Jase. The sudden feelings of jealousy that filled Ali left her shaken. She tried to tamp down her reaction to another woman in Jase's life, and she knew that was just the beginning. Tamping down her feelings for Jase would be even harder, though she'd gotten a head start on that when she got the call exposing him.

"Mr. VanDam is on the telephone at the moment," the secretary explained with a smile, "but Frank Wilson asked me to show you to the conference room where they will meet with you. And I'll tell Mr. VanDam's assistant you're here."

Ali thanked her and followed her down the hall. She read the labels on the closed doors they passed but saw none that would identify one as Jase's office.

"Would you like a cup of coffee?" the secretary

asked when they reached the conference room. Ali declined. "Well, I'll leave you here then. You can sit anywhere you like. Mr. Wilson will be right up."

"I'm here now," Wilson said, coming into the room behind her. He thanked the secretary, who left the room, and greeted Ali. "I'm so glad you were able to come in this morning. I like working with someone who wants to get going on the new job right away," he said with a broad smile on his face.

He and Ali shook hands, and then he asked, "Won't you sit down? Mr. VanDam will be here to join us directly. He just arrived from checking the new bakery and wanted to take a moment to check his phone messages first."

Fortifying her resolve to remain calm with a deep breath, Ali walked to the opposite side of the large table, determined to be facing the door when Jase walked in. She had just dropped her purse and briefcase onto the second chair when Jase appeared at the door. He was looking down at pink sheets of phone messages as he entered the room.

In his own corporate offices as the company's owner, he looked very distinguished and powerful in a gray double-breasted suit, his tie tight around his crisp collar, his stubborn hair orderly. His appearance shocked Ali, as if she'd been doused with a pail of cold water. She gripped the back of the chair in front of her when her knees threatened to give way.

"Sorry to keep you waiting, Frank," Jase said absently. He continued reading the notes while he shut the door. He turned and finally glanced up from the sheets to nod at Wilson, and then he looked at Ali. His eyes widened and his mouth dropped open as if he were about to speak, but no sound came out.

Wilson stepped into the awkward silence and introduced the two of them. Their gazes still locked, neither of them moved.

"How could you do this, Jase?" Ali whispered hoarsely after a few moments.

Wilson frowned and dropped his pen on the table. "Ah . . . You know each other? Well . . . ah . . . Why don't we sit down and . . ."

"How could you lie to me?" Ali interrupted.

"Ali, you're the one who got the contract?" Jase asked. He glanced at Wilson, who nodded, and then back at her. "I didn't know it went to you until just this minute. I swear. Tell her, Frank."

"Ah, yes," Wilson put in. "Mr. VanDam chose not to be a part of the selection process." He looked at Ali expectantly, but she didn't take her gaze from Jase.

"You knew I applied and now you expect me to believe you didn't even ask about my chances?" Ali drew her lips between her teeth and bit down on them. Her heart was pounding.

"I wanted to, but I couldn't. I had to stay neutral."

Ali shook her head in disbelief.

"Ms. deGroot?" Wilson prompted. "If we can all sit down, we can talk this out." He pulled out his chair, but the other two did not follow suit.

"I promise you, I didn't know it was you." Jase tossed the pink notes on the table. "I had no idea who got the contract."

Ali pointed an index finger at him. "You're the owner of the whole company and you claim you didn't know who got the contract? What kind of owner doesn't know something as important as who is going to handle his company's promotional event?"

"I couldn't let you think I was responsible, no matter how it turned out."

"I assure you, Ms. deGroot, that Mr. VanDam did not know who was awarded the contract. The decision was mine," Wilson insisted. "Now then. Ah . . . Ms. deGroot, it would be appropriate at this initial meeting for you to give Mr. VanDam an overview of your plans for the bakery opening."

Ali looked at Wilson, trying to decide if she could believe him and wishing he'd stop talking about the promotion. She jerked her head back when Jase spoke.

"I should have told you, Ali. I wanted to, and I tried, in fact. Every day since you told me you submitted a bid."

"So why didn't you?" Ali asked, the hurt she felt weakening her voice.

"Each time I looked at you, at your eyes, you were so trusting, so sweet. I couldn't . . . I just couldn't find the right moment. I didn't want to disappoint you." Jase ran his hand through his hair and the stubborn strand in front fell across his forehead.

"So you had Mr. Wilson here call me about the contract instead? You knew I would find out then. Was that easier for you than you telling me? Or did you think that giving me the contract would be such a big boon for my little business that it would smooth everything over? I'd be so grateful, right? Soften me up for your big move?" Ali asked much less quietly as she leaned on her fingertips on the table. "And if I hadn't applied, you never would have told me. You would have gone right on lying to me about who you are until you got what you wanted from me or gave up trying."

Jase leaned over his side of the table in a mirror image of her stance. Their faces were only a couple of feet apart. "That isn't the way it was at all. Please, Ali. I didn't have a thing to do with awarding the contract," Jase told her firmly. "That was his doing entirely," he added as he straightened, with a jerk of his thumb in Wilson's direction.

"Mr. VanDam asked me to . . ." Wilson began.

"You deliberately deceived me, Jase." Ali straightened. "Okay, so maybe you didn't engineer my getting the promotions bid, but you listened to me talk about it, and you let me go on and on about how excited I was at the possibility of handling the promotion. How could you do that?"

"Ali, I didn't know what to do. Once I decided to tell you, I didn't know how."

"How could you say *nothing*? You didn't even try to tell me." Her hands shook as she picked up her purse and briefcase. "Here I thought it would be fun to work where you worked because you're fun to be with and if our paths crossed there . . ." She shrugged. "And you spoke so highly of the people working for the company." She stared at him. "I guess I was stupid, but I never even guessed you owned the whole company. You made a fool of me!"

"Ali, I'm so sorry and I want to explain."

"No, thank you." She shook her head and walked around a decidedly pale Wilson at the end of the table. "Oh, I'll bet you got a good laugh out of the whole thing, didn't you? No wonder you left my house so fast after I told you about submitting a proposal for the promotion. It wasn't that you didn't like my ideas, was it?"

She raised a hand to stop him from responding. "Hey, maybe I should congratulate you. You sure fooled me. I thought you were a baker, an errand boy, but you're not, are you? You're a great deal more, and you wanted to keep that information from me."

She stopped a foot from Jase, who had crossed to the door to intercept her. "You couldn't even be honest with me, couldn't even trust me with knowing who you are. How do you think that makes me feel?" she asked more loudly, venting more of her anger and hurt. "Our whole relationship is like a fairy tale that begins with 'Once upon a lie.' "

"Ms. deGroot, if there is a problem . . ." Wilson put in weakly.

Jase reached to hold her shoulders as she turned to leave. She tried to pull free from his grasp, but he wouldn't let her escape. "Ali, the last thing in the whole world I want to do is hurt you," he said softly. His grip softened and he circled his thumbs on her shoulders.

She willed herself not to react to his warm touch. "Well, maybe you should have thought of that a long time ago—the first time we met," she whispered. She looked at him only a moment longer before she twisted out of his grip and opened the door to the meeting room.

"Where do you think you're going?" Jase asked.

She glanced back at him over her shoulder. "I'm going home, but anywhere to get away from here would be better than staying. I've had all of you and Dutch Treats that I can stomach."

Wilson gasped as his head whipped back and forth, watching them as he would a tennis match.

Jase took two quick strides to the door and raised his arm to the jamb beyond her shoulder, effectively stopping her exit. He ran his other hand through his hair and dropped it to rest on his hip. He glanced over at Wilson and then looked back at her. "Look," he said, working to keep his voice steady and quiet. "This isn't the place to discuss this. Please come into my office, where we can have some privacy."

"No, I won't. I don't want to be in an office alone with you, Jase. I don't want to be alone with you anywhere," Ali said with more force than she probably should have, given the circumstances. But tears were stinging in her eyes and she wanted to get out while she could still hold them at bay.

"Okay, then, Frank, would you excuse us?" Jase asked with a quick glance in his direction.

"No," Ali insisted, holding her hand up to stop Wilson from leaving. "I meant it. I don't want to be here or anywhere alone with you, Jase. We have nothing left to discuss about our relationship or about this job. I'm leaving."

"Mr. VanDam, I'll . . ."

Wilson didn't have a chance. This time he was interrupted by Jase's assistant, who appeared at the door behind him. She looked frightened. Jase dropped his arm from the doorjamb and turned to her as she spoke.

"Excuse me," she said in a worried voice. "The Liverpool shop is on the phone. You've got to take the call. Quick. Please," she pleaded.

Jase loped over to pick up the phone from the secretary's desk outside the conference room. Ali trailed out behind his assistant. Wilson followed in her wake.

"I'll be right there as fast as I can," Jase said into the phone and slapped it down into the cradle. "Roxie, I need a ride to Liverpool—as fast as we can get there! I'll explain on the way."

While Roxie pulled her purse from a desk drawer

and jogged across the office, Jase strode over to Ali and held her shoulders again. "You and I are not done discussing this," he told her. Then he ran out the door, with Roxie right behind him.

Ali heard their footsteps echo down the stairs. They hadn't even waited for the elevator.

Wilson stepped over to her side. "Um. Ms. deGroot, I'm sorry that Mr. VanDam was called away. Why don't we reschedule this meeting?" he asked cheerfully, as if he hadn't just witnessed Ali's life falling apart.

"No. No, thank you, Mr. Wilson. I'm declining your offer for the contract. You'll need to find someone else to do the promotion."

Ali turned and walked out of the office on trembling legs, leaving Wilson in stunned silence.

Chapter Nine

Jase took off his coat and vest and tossed them in the backseat of Roxie's car along with his tie. Roxie had the car started by the time he climbed in the front, but as they headed for the crosstown highway, he felt that she wasn't driving fast enough. But he didn't complain. She was driving faster than her usual pace and getting a ride with her was a whole lot faster than waiting for a taxi. Right now, getting to the bakery was the most important thing.

"Hey, fasten your seatbelt." Jase did as Roxie ordered. "Thanks. Now I can take the corners faster," she said with a grin.

"You can't take them fast enough for me on this trip as long as you're careful."

"Now you wouldn't be telling me to go faster than the legal limit, would you, boss?"

Jase held onto the dashboard with both hands as they sailed down the on ramp.

"Do you want to tell me if heading for Liverpool as fast as we can, hopefully without getting stopped for speeding, has anything to do with the shouting in the office just before we left?" she asked, not taking her eyes off the road.

"You could hear it, huh?" Jase asked.

Roxie shrugged as her tires spun as they sped up to join the highway traffic. "I thought I recognized her from somewhere. Is she working for you at one of the retail outlets?"

Jase sighed audibly. "No. Wilson offered her the promotions job. This was the opportunity to meet me and go over the plans." He grabbed the armrest as Roxie took a sharp curve.

"She must not have taken a shine to you, boss. From the anger level in her voice, I'd guess she took exception to the offer."

"You could say that." He leaned forward to see the highway signs. "This is our exit coming up."

"Got it, boss." She snapped on her turn signal and steered into the exit-only lane.

"You were right about Ali, though. Saying that you recognized her, I mean. She's my next-door neighbor. You probably saw her in her yard or somewhere one of the times you brought me home."

"Yeah, that was it. She's cute."

"I can't argue with that."

"So what's the problem? Didn't she want the job?" Roxie glanced in his direction. "Or don't you want me to ask? Just tell me if it's none of my business."

"No, that's okay. As my assistant you'll find out anyway. You see, when Wilson called her to grant her the contract, he also mentioned that I would be meeting with her. Ah, and he mentioned that I owned the company."

"Aaaahh! Now it falls into place. I remember you telling me you didn't want anyone in the new neighborhood to know who you were."

"Yeah. I never told Ali and we've been dating. It sort of backfired on me."

"Sort of? I seem to remember we had a conversation about the possibility of this situation arising. It was in your backyard, if my memory serves."

"Don't remind me."

"So she doesn't understand why you wanted to lie to her?"

Jase groaned. "Don't call it a lie. I never wanted to lie to her. It sounds terrible when you say it that way."

"But I'll bet she sees it as a lie."

Jase ran his hands over his face. "Got that in one. And then the call from Liverpool. What a day."

Roxie pulled onto the street where the Liverpool bakery was located. "Say, you never told me why we're heading to this bakery at breakneck speed."

She neared the building and slowed to a stop. A police car was parked diagonally across the street. "Oh, no. You don't have to now." She turned to Jase, who was staring out through the windshield. "I can see for myself why we're here," she said more softly.

Jase looked over at her. "Can you come in while I assess the damage? We can decide what to do and then you can head back to the office and begin the PR damage control."

"You don't want me to stick around to take you back?"

"No, it'll be a while and I probably won't get back to the office today. I'll find another way home when I'm done here."

Roxie pulled over and parked her car as close to the bakery as she could. She and Jase jumped out of the car and jogged the rest of the way.

A policeman stopped them at the parking lot. "Can't go in there today, folks. The bakery is closed."

"Not to us," Jase said with authority. "I own the place and this is my assistant."

The officer checked his identification and waved them on through. Jase ran toward the building with Roxie right behind him.

Ali rose from the chaise on her deck, where she'd been going over ad copy for the newspaper. She thought she'd heard a car in the driveway. Peering over the fence, she saw that at least her hearing had not deceived her.

She watched as the driver, a woman Ali judged to be in her late forties, climbed out and opened the back door of the car. Ali recognized her as the one who had left with Jase that morning.

The woman lifted out a small pile of folded clothes and settled it on one arm. Then she saw Ali watching her. "Hi," she called out in a friendly voice, with a wave. "I was hoping you'd be home."

Ali felt embarrassed for having been spying on her every move. "Hi," she responded more weakly. "I didn't mean to be nosy, I just thought . . ." She stopped because she wasn't sure just what she had thought.

"Not a problem. Jase won't be home for a while, but it's nice to know that he lives in an area where people care about their neighbors."

Ali felt the cold fingers of deception squeeze her heart again. If only she knew how much, she thought.

Instead of going into Jase's house, the woman turned and walked toward Ali. Not particularly wanting to continue the conversation, but feeling it would be rude to turn her back on her, Ali opened the gate and stepped out to meet her on the driveway.

"I'm Roxanne Warner, but please call me Roxie. I didn't get a chance to meet you at the office this morning because of our fast exit."

"Oh, you know who I am then," Ali said. She looked at the bundle Roxie held and realized it was the suit that Jase had been wearing that morning.

"I'm just bringing it home for him. He took it off the minute we got to the Liverpool store and stuck on a uniform so he wouldn't ruin this." She shook her head and smiled. "My husband thinks I'm nuts for all that I do for Jase, but I think it's the mother instinct in me. He's only eight or nine years older than my oldest. I have three kids, by the way," she inserted with a proud grin.

Ali nodded and smiled in return. She really didn't want to be standing in the driveway listening to all this woman did for Jase.

"I could have left his suit at the office, but I thought I could leave it with you on my way back there. Then Jase could get it from you . . . Well, you get my plan."

Ali nodded. "Sure, I suppose, but I don't know when I'll see him next."

"Well, I can tell him you have it, and then he'll stop by for it. It's not as if you two could live next door and never see each other," she said with a chuckle.

And that was exactly what Ali had been worried about. The editing she was doing on her ads was taking forever because she couldn't concentrate on them. She kept thinking about Jase and how sad she felt that what they had was gone. She gave herself a mental shake.

"I guess I don't understand how it would be ruined just hanging at the bakery somewhere until he could bring the suit home himself."

"The smell, and it might get wet," Roxie answered simply. Ali frowned. "From the fire."

"Fire? I had no idea there was a fire." Ali's heart sped up with worry.

"Oh, I thought you would have heard about it on the radio by now."

Ali shook her head. "No, I haven't heard a word. I convinced my sister, who's visiting me from Chicago, to get out of the house and go shopping for the afternoon. Since she drove to the mall, I've been trying to work and I haven't had a radio or television on. Was anyone injured? Was the fire damage extensive?"

"No one was hurt, thank goodness. They were still deciding what the damage was when I left. The building is okay. I know that much, but I don't know about the equipment inside. You'll have to hear about that from Jase."

"Oh, well, I probably won't have the opportunity to—"

"Sure you will. He's got to come get his suit, remember? Here."

She handed Ali the suit. Catching it against her chest with both arms so she didn't drop anything, she smelled the spicy fragrance of his aftershave. Her throat swelled and she swallowed hard to clear it.

"I should hang this up. Would you like to come in for a glass of iced tea or something?"

"Thanks. That would be nice to wash the smoke out of my throat."

After getting a suit hanger, Ali hung the suit on the coat hook beside the kitchen door and fixed their drinks. A few minutes later, they were settled on the padded chairs on the deck with their glasses of tea.

"You know, I saw your proposal for the promotion at the new store. Frank Wilson showed it to me because he was so impressed with its originality and creativity. You had some very good ideas. Compared to the others that looked like copycat plans taken from what they'd seen on television, yours was easily the winner. Personally, I think Frank is lucky to have found you."

"Oh, but you don't understand . . ."

"Well, I wasn't in on the decision-making, of course. That's not my job. I'm Jase's executive assistant. Sounds good, doesn't it? My husband was impressed. What it means is that I work hard, but not as long and hard as Jase does. And let me tell you, I was so happy when Frank told me Jase was letting him handle the selection of the winner from the bids that came in. I can't tell you what a relief it was for me."

Ali shook her head. "Now I'm the one who doesn't understand."

"Well, to explain I have to go back a long way—six years, in fact. I started working for Jase when he was getting started. After my kids were in school, I went back to earn an MBA. Jase needed someone with business knowledge to carry out his orders and to keep the big picture in mind. Then while he was working on the details, I would keep track of everything else that had to be done so he wouldn't forget anything." She sipped her tea and shook her head. "It should have been sort of the other way around. He drove me nuts at first and I almost quit."

"What do you mean?" Ali asked, but she had the feeling Roxie didn't need the prompt to continue.

"Well, to put it in my daughter's words, he was a 'control freak.' " She laughed. "Still is. He has to do everything himself. And I do mean everything. He was practically telling each shop how many cookies to make chocolate and how many to make vanilla instead of letting the managers decide themselves from the sales record in their own shop."

"I can understand that feeling. Time and time again I feel that if I don't do it myself, it won't get done right."

"And maybe that works for a one-person operation, but when you expand, you'll see what I mean," Roxie said easily. "Jase was working himself way too hard. With each new store, he seemed to spend more time at work. Lately, I think it's been affecting his health. For one thing, he's lost weight."

Ali thought he looked good, but agreed that he had no extra weight on him. "Working days and some nights too can't be good for him."

"That's for sure. So when he told Frank Wilson that analyzing the promotion bids and granting the contract was entirely up to him, I almost jumped up and cheered. I thought Jase was finally trusting someone else to do the job they were hired for—and without him telling them how to do it. It did wonders for Frank too. He's very knowledgeable, but if you don't let people know that you trust them to do what they're supposed to, they lose confidence in themselves."

Ali leaned back in her chair and sighed. Roxie

sipped her tea and set the glass on the small table between them.

"I couldn't help but hear the conversation you two were having in the conference room this morning. I . . . well, I feel sort of responsible for the problems between you and Jase."

Ali sat up and looked at her. "You? How could you possibly feel responsible?"

Roxie turned a little in her chair to face Ali directly. "I didn't push the point that I thought he shouldn't do it."

Ali frowned. "I beg your pardon?"

"One evening weeks ago when I brought Jase home, we got to talking about his house and this neighborhood. He told me how much he liked working in the garden, and he even told me about his cute neighbor—you."

She smiled. Ali tried to say something, but Roxie wouldn't let her interrupt.

" 'Course, at the time, he didn't even know if you were married or anything." Roxie smiled and continued. "I knew from what he said that one of the reasons he'd moved here was to make a clean break from his previous relationships. On top of working hard, he dated women who expected him to play hard. So he was taking them to all the right places, but he wasn't enjoying any of it. Putting up a big expensive party front isn't Jase. He comes from a nice hard-working family. His parents would rather add to their grandchildren's college funds than go on a fancy vacation at a resort. They're good people. And so is Jase."

"But what didn't you tell him to do?"

"Well, he bought this place as a hideout. Here he hoped he could be just plain Jase VanDam, hard worker, nice guy, and no more special for any reason than the next guy. He said he didn't want people here to find out he owned the chain of bakeries because they would look at him in a different light. They wouldn't see him as the man he really was. I think he wanted to meet a woman who could like him for the person he is and not for the money he may have or any business he may own."

"And you didn't tell him not to keep the secret."

"Yeah. I told him it wasn't like him not to be completely honest with people. He insisted that he didn't think it could hurt anyone. But it did—big time. I know he's hurting and now I can see you are too."

Ali lowered her gaze to the glass in her hand. "Yeah, you could say that."

Roxie smiled kindly. "So I used the suit as an excuse to come and say I'm sorry. I think the world of Jase, and he's been a different man lately—a happy man—and I think that's all due to you."

Tears burned at the backs of Ali's eyes. She blinked and looked away. There was nothing she could say. She didn't owe Roxie any explanation, but she did appreciate her coming. "Thanks for stopping by to tell me. Jase is lucky to have you working for him."

"Well, thanks for the tea. And speaking of work, I'd better get back there." She rose and Ali followed her across the yard to the driveway. "Jase is a good man. And the business he's built from the ground up is good too." She grinned. "With you to do the promotion, nothing could be better," she concluded.

Ali drew in a gulp of air.

"Say, we've never had to reopen a shop after a fire, but maybe the reopening will be in time for the grand opening of the new store. We could promote the two at once. Ah, but that's your department now, not mine."

Roxie led the way to the driveway, where she climbed into her car and started the engine. "Thanks for giving the suit to Jase. I'll tell him I gave it to you. He'll probably stop in on his way home to get it." She winked. "If my plan works, he will anyway. Gosh, I hope he isn't too late with the mess at the bakery," she rattled on. "Well, nice meeting you," she added as she slammed the car door and backed down the driveway.

"You too," Ali responded, trying to smile and wondering how the conversation could have gone on for so long without making Roxie understand that she'd declined the offer of the promotions contract with Dutch Treats.

Chapter Ten

Near to midnight Jase climbed out of the taxi in his driveway. After paying the driver, he noticed that Ali's kitchen light was on. Crossing the driveway, he knocked softly on her door. He'd planned to wait until the next day to see her at a more reasonable hour, after he'd had time to clean up, but he needed to see her now. He couldn't wait.

She opened the door quickly. He noticed the mug and paperback book set upside down on the kitchen table and concluded she must have been waiting up for him. He took that as a good sign. And the way he felt, he needed to focus on something good right now.

She came to the door wrapped up in a terrycloth robe and comfortable-looking moccasin slippers. She

132

unhooked the screen for him and stepped back without a word.

Jase trudged in and leaned against the kitchen counter. His white shirt was covered with black smudges, and he stank of acrid smoke. He couldn't ever remember feeling so tired in his whole life. He knew Ali's counter was holding him upright.

"Do you want to sit down?" she asked tentatively.

"I'd better not. I'm dirty and my pants are still wet from the knees down."

He hadn't expected a warm welcome, but when Ali stood there looking at him without saying another word, it hurt him. And as he looked into her amazing eyes at that moment, he knew that she could hurt him deeply, because without ever intending to, he'd fallen in love with her. The realization gave him a surge of energy, which he used to explain what had happened at the bakery.

"There was a fire in the rotating oven," he began.

Ali nodded. "Yes. How did it happen?"

"They're not sure if the temperature gauge was off, or if something went wrong with the burners. The smoke from the rolls on fire inside, plus the gaskets burning, set off the alarm. The heat triggered the sprinklers. They sprayed water on everything for a long time before the firemen got there and shut them off."

"Is it over?"

Jase nodded his head slowly and closed his eyes. He

had trouble getting them to open again. "The fire department made sure the fire was out. Everything was ruined, even though the fire itself was contained in the oven."

"Thank goodness it wasn't worse."

"I'm thankful the staff thought fast enough to turn off the gas and keep the oven doors shut. The fire would have burned itself out eventually when the rolls were chunks of charcoal. But the whole bakery is blackened inside from the smoke that poured through the cracks in the door. Everything smells burned from the fire and is soggy and dirty from the sprinklers."

"Jase, I'm so sorry," Ali whispered in a hoarse voice. She made no move to wipe the tears that overflowed from her eyes.

Jase wanted to hold her more than he ever had before. He wanted to comfort her and dry her tears. He needed her comforting hug to wash away his own pain and tension. But after what had happened today at the office, he didn't dare touch her. He didn't know if he ever could again.

She made no move toward him. He felt as if they were miles apart instead of a few feet. He'd lost her because he'd deceived her. And then he'd come close to losing everything he'd worked so hard and long for at his store. Now he was too exhausted to think.

"The bakery is closed until I get it cleaned up and put in a new oven. We started mopping up today, but I sent everyone home to get some sleep. We'll go back again tomorrow."

"Is it just repainting and replacing the oven?"

"No, I'll have to get all new supplies because the heavy smoke and water everywhere contaminated what's stored there now." Jase inhaled deeply and released the air with a shudder. "Then the whole operation has to be re-inspected before the shop can gear up to open for business again." He rested his head against the upper cabinet and closed his eyes.

"Jase, you're so tired you can hardly stand up. Do you want something to drink?"

He shook his head and straightened. "No, that's not what I need right now."

His gaze met hers and she looked down at her hands, knotted at her waist. He tried to stand on his own two feet without the counter's help. He wavered. She reached out as if to help him and then quickly withdrew her arm before she touched him. Jase knew his only option and stepped toward the door.

"Is the bakery really going to be okay?" Ali asked.

"I have a gigantic cleanup over the next couple weeks, but yeah. It'll be okay." Jase stopped, his hand on the doorknob. "Ali . . ."

He looked into her wide eyes. She looked worried about him and the bakery. That had to mean that she hadn't written him off completely, didn't it? "Ah, well, I just wanted to tell you what happened before I went home to get some sleep."

"Sure. Thanks. Thanks for stopping by. I'll tell Helen all about it." She lifted down his suit and handed it to him. "I put it on a hanger after Roxie left it here, but you'll want to get it cleaned before you wear it again. There are stains and water marks. I hope they come out."

"I'm sure they will." He paused until she lifted her gaze to meet his. "I didn't know she was bringing it here, Ali. I told her I'd get it from her tomorrow. I just didn't want it to sit at the bakery and soak up the smells of the fire."

"It's okay. No bother."

"What I'm trying to say is that I think Roxie brought it here to give me an excuse to talk to you again."

Ali nodded. "Yeah. I can see that she's worried about you."

"She's more than an assistant. She's a good friend."

"Oh, I have this for you too." She stepped over to the table and picked up a white handkerchief. "All clean and pressed," she added as she handed it to him. Had she held it by the corner so as not to touch his hand, or was that his imagination? He was too tired to tell, but she had not touched him. Not once tonight.

"Thanks."

"I guess that's everything," she concluded as she looked out the door, dismissing him.

Jase didn't want that to be the end. He wanted to pick up where they'd left off in his office, but he didn't have the strength. With a "good night," he went home. He'd been awake for forty hours. He could hardly think straight and had to get some rest before he fell asleep on his feet. The cleanup would start early in the morning.

When his alarm went off six hours later, he felt as if he'd just flopped down on the bed. He dragged himself up and got ready to go supervise the cleanup. As he stood in the driveway waiting for the taxi, he studied Ali's house. There were no signs that anyone was awake yet.

"Don't hate me too much, Ali," he whispered. "I never meant to hurt you."

The taxi rolled to a stop in front of him. Jase climbed in and told the driver where to go. "Oh, and wake me up a little before you get there so I can at least look awake when I walk in the door," he added before he leaned back in the corner of the seat and promptly fell asleep.

The insurance adjuster arrived at the bakery first thing that morning. "None of the other equipment has been damaged, but the smoke and water damage means all the surfaces will have to be cleaned and then everything painted," he told Jase. "Other than your deductible, you're covered."

Never one to leave the work to others, Jase pitched in to help. He couldn't arrange for anyone else to come in any sooner to do the work, but he knew it meant it would be a while before he would have time to talk to Ali.

If she would ever talk to him again.

Ali tossed and turned after finally getting to bed after Jase left just past midnight. One minute she was glad she'd waited up to learn exactly what happened with the fire. The next she was angry with herself for caring so much that she had waited up. If he hadn't seen her light . . . She groaned and vowed for the umpteenth time to quit thinking about him.

Sleep finally came and didn't leave until later than usual. She pulled on jeans and a blouse after a quick shower and still hadn't figured out how to distance herself from her feelings. The more she cared, the more it hurt. It would take time, she knew.

Helen was in the kitchen cleaning up her few breakfast dishes when Ali joined her and shared the terrible news.

"Oh, Ali, Jase must be beside himself. Is there anything we can do to help?"

"That was my first thought too. And all night I've tried to talk myself out of it! I'm probably being stupid on top of foolish, but I'm going to run over to the bakery after I eat something. The cleanup must be awful after the automatic sprinklers soaked everything. There must be something I can do to help. I mean, that's what neighbors are for, right?"

"Neighbors? Oh, hon. You really care for him, don't you?" Helen opened her arms to her sister, who returned the warm hug.

"Yeah, and that's why his deception hurts so much."

"I think helping out if we can is a good idea. So count me in. I'm going to the shop too," Helen announced as she jumped up to get dressed. "I'll be ready in five minutes."

Ali gulped down toast and coffee and they left. She

found a parking space down the block from the bakery building after passing the congested parking lot. "Will you look at those huge fans in the doorways drawing out the stench?" Helen said.

"The smell of burned bread and sugar is only slightly better than the smell of burned oven gaskets," Ali replied.

The women walked through the door and saw the white walls near the ovens streaked with black and the ceiling turned dark gray. Signs that had been hanging on the wall over each rack or basket were curled and blurred after the dousing from the sprinklers. The water-based paint used for the lettering ran down the smoke-smudged walls in red and blue streams below them.

The huge metal racks and baskets that had held rolls and loaves of bread were empty already and pushed against the front windows. The former delicious occupants of those racks, including all the matching wicker baskets, had been dumped in a heap on the wet tile floor.

Using grain shovels with high sides to contain the liquid, Jase and two other men were shoveling the soggy baked goods into heavy-duty garbage cans sitting in the center of the bakery showroom. With every toss, water splashed out, soaking the men and everything around them.

When the cans were full, two of the men took turns and pulled them across the floor and out the door to a garbage bin parked near the entrance. The water tipped with the baked goods into the large containers ran down and escaped through cracks at the bottom, wetting the ground at the edge of the blacktopped lot where they sat.

Ali stepped tentatively inside the door, and Jase walked over to her and Helen immediately. He looked exhausted, wet, and dirty. Ali guessed that what looked like mud smeared on his clothes was most likely chocolate. Roxie had been right, she thought. He did look thinner than he did weeks before when he had moved in next door.

"Hi. You okay?" Ali asked. "Ah . . . We came to help. . . . We're neighbors, after all," she added awkwardly, with a little shrug.

Jase stared at her a moment and then nodded. "Come see the mess. Helen, you've got to believe me when I say this is not the tour of my bakery that I had in mind when I told you I'd show you around." He managed a smile.

"I'll take the tour later. Tell us what to do so we can pitch right in to help," Helen responded.

"Okay, here's what you can do." He pulled one of the big empty plastic garbage cans over to the showcase and slid open the glass doors on the back of each one. "Empty the shelves and toss everything in, one tray at a time or a cake at a time, whatever you want."

"But the pies, the cakes, and those baskets of delicious-looking cookies in the glass cases aren't even wet," Helen said, a hopeful note in her voice.

"Those brownies make my mouth water. Do you have to throw them out?" Ali asked.

"Sadly, yes. None of it is fit for consumption after the smoke from the fire hitting it. We have no idea of the toxins that might have been in the smoke."

The women sadly began work at once and Jase went back to shoveling. Ali lifted the trays one at a time and Helen pushed the sweet treats into the garbage can. As soon as they filled a can, one of the men took it out and dumped it while they started to fill the next.

"What a terrible waste!" Helen exclaimed.

"That's the understatement of the day," Ali responded.

"It sure took a lot shorter time to throw it all out than it did to create it. Besides being a waste, it's all so depressing."

The professional cleaning service Jase had hired finally arrived just before they had the last of the baked goods thrown out. Everyone helped pull the row of tall empty racks out the shop door into the parking lot so the cleaning crew could vacuum up the remaining water puddled on the tiles. After the wall, ceilings, and floors were clean, they would have to steam-clean and disinfect everything before they put it back in place. It would take them more than a few hours. That was certain.

Standing in the parking lot as the service took over the work, Ali took one look at Helen in the daylight and was worried. "You don't look so good. Are you feeling okay?"

Helen smiled weakly. "That food wasn't exactly appetizing and the smell started to get to me. I just feel a little queasy. That's all. I'm not ill. Just let me get some more fresh air a minute. I'll be fine."

Jase had walked up just as Helen was giving her explanation. "Listen, you just need a change of scenery. This place is a mess, but thanks to you both we've gotten the last of the food out before the cleaning crew arrived. They've already begun scrubbing the walls and ceilings. So you see, there isn't anything left for you two to do."

"We'll go then," Ali concluded. "I'll take Helen home."

Jase walked with them to Ali's car. "I can't thank you enough for coming."

"I wish there was more we could do to help you, Jase," Helen told him. Ali thought she already looked better. Getting some lunch would make them both feel even better.

"Thanks," Jase responded as Helen turned toward her side of the car.

"I . . . We hate to see you hurting," Ali said. She longed to put her arms around him and give him what measure of comfort she could. But he might misunderstand her intentions. Instead, she turned away to the car.

"Me too," he whispered behind her. She stopped and glanced over her shoulder at him. The pain in his face was clearly evident despite his attempt at a smile.

"So long," he said more loudly, with a wave to both

of them. "And thanks again. I'll . . . ah . . . let you know how it goes."

Ali nodded and climbed in behind the wheel. As she and Helen fastened their seatbelts, Ali watched Jase walk back down the block. She couldn't help but notice that his shoulders were drooped instead of in their usual straight posture.

A picture of her father walking almost identically flashed into her mind. "You know, Helen, I saw that same tired, stooped look on Dad." Ali steered the car out from the parking space. "All the times Dad missed my school programs or recitals, I always thought he was being inconsiderate or just didn't love me enough to come." She turned onto the road to the state highway that would take them home.

"Ali, you must know now that wasn't the case. He had a responsibility to his employees as well as to his family."

"Yeah. As an adult, I can see that the division of his time called for impossible decisions. And I'm sorry. I don't think I ever really understood until now."

Ali sighed, comfortable with her understanding after looking at her father's work from a new point of view. "And when he had to decide which one to sacrifice, his business or his family, in order to spend time on the other, he must have spent the time on the one that needed him the most at that moment. It's no wonder he felt stressed most of the time."

"It can't have been easy to decide. He must have always wondered if he could have done more for both."

"But, Helen, sometimes he ignored the family when we really needed him."

"I know. I missed having him around too." Helen smiled. "Dad couldn't have worked so hard without Mom's help. Kinda sad that Jase has no one special to help and support him other than employees."

Ali refused to reply to Helen's pointed comment, but she had to agree. She checked the rearview mirror before turning into her driveway. There she pushed her thoughts of Jase to the attic of her mind, wishing her pain could be easily forgotten. For the time being she had lots to do and was counting on keeping busy so she wouldn't think about Jase.

She didn't want any free time to think about how she'd fallen in love with a man who was a Mr. Not Right, or about how much it had hurt her to walk away.

Chapter Eleven

Ali pulled in the driveway and parked at her kitchen door the next morning. She'd run to the store for a few groceries and fresh produce for herself and Helen.

"I'll get those for you," Jase said from behind her when she lifted the bags from behind her seat.

Ali shook her head. "No need," she said, her voice husky with emotion. "Thanks, but they're not heavy." She tried to step around him.

"Wait." Jase held up his hand and grasped her upper arm gently to stop her. "Please. Hear me out."

Not wanting to be outright rude, Ali paused with a little nod. He took the grocery bags from her hands.

"I shouldn't have been less than completely honest with you, and I'm sorry I was. More sorry than I can say."

Ali nodded and tried to turn away, but he held her arm.

"I've been thinking a lot about us because you're very important to me, and, well, I have the feeling that what's gone wrong between us has to do with more than just the fact I didn't let on who I really was."

"Now wait . . ."

"Please. Just let me finish. Before you got the promotions job, I think we'd come to care about each other."

Unable to meet his gaze because he was right, Ali looked down at the driveway.

"But the more I thought about what happened after you found me out, the more confused I got. I would have expected that you'd be glad I was the owner and not a baker and handyman. I figured my little lie should have caused us a little embarrassment the first time we met in my office, but then we should have laughed over it and been finished with it. This has gone way farther than that."

"Jase, I'm angry at you. You made a fool out of me."

Despite the grocery-bag handles looped over his palms, he reached for Ali's shoulders and held them gently. "No, honey. No one considers you a fool. And I don't think your anger was all my fault. I have a hunch that you're mixing up your annoyance at my fib with the anger you still feel toward your former fiancé who lied to you."

He was hitting too close to home—on everything. She tried to twist out of his grasp, but he held her in place. Ali blinked against the tears welling in her eyes.

"Aw, honey. I don't want to upset you, but I'd like

you to believe that I'm not the guy who lied and stole your money." Jase couldn't help himself. He pulled her close and wrapped his arms around her to give her whatever comfort she wanted to take from his hug. "You deserve so much better than him."

Jase savored the moments with her in his arms. When she raised her arms, tentatively placed them at his waist, and rested her head on his shoulder, he wanted to shout for joy. "But he's long gone. And good riddance." He loosened his hold to allow her to tip up her head so he could look at her face. "And you can be sure that I'm not after your money. And I'm not going to lie ever again."

She sighed and looked down at his shirtfront. "Maybe you're right, Jase," she said without raising her head again to meet his gaze. "I don't know. Maybe I have been more angry with you than I should have been."

Jase kissed the top of her head. "All I ask is that you think about it. I care a great deal for you, Ali, and I want you to be a big part of my life." He took a deep breath. "I don't want to lose you."

When she looked up then, he saw tears streaming down her cheeks. He put both grocery bags in one hand and pulled out his handkerchief to pat them dry before he tucked it into one of her hands.

"You keep loaning these to me. Maybe I should buy some of my own," she joked. "They're a lot better than tissues."

"You're welcome to all of mine that you need." Jase smiled. "Feel better?"

"Yes. And I'll think about it, Jase."

"Good. As long as we're thinking and talking about our problems, I know we can solve them."

She nodded and turned toward her house. "I'd better go see how Helen is."

"Is she feeling better than at the shop?"

Nodding, Ali said, "She just felt so nauseated this morning that she stayed home."

"Is it the flu?"

"I think she's depressed and feels miserable that Eric hasn't called once since she got here, but he may not even know yet that she's here. She's kinda caught."

"Tell her I said hello," Jase said, handing her the grocery bags. "And thank you for thinking about what happened between us, Ali. When we're both back on an even keel, I need you to tell me you forgive me."

Jase watched as she nodded once and turned to unlock her door. He stayed where he was until she'd closed it behind her. She'd never looked back at him, not even a glance. He sighed heavily and went into his own house for the papers he'd come home to get.

Ali answered the kitchen extension phone on the second ring to hear a worried Eric. "Hi, Eric. I'm so glad you called." Ali spoke deliberately loud for Helen to hear. She immediately came right over to stand at her side.

"Ali, what's going on?" Eric asked in a worried tone. "Is Helen okay? I came home in the middle of the night to find her gone. I didn't know a thing about her planning to go see you. I called the office this morning, and if she hadn't told them where she was, I never would have known. I've been frantic all night with worry."

"Eric, she's standing right here. I'll let you talk to her."

Ali handed the phone to Helen with her hand covering the mouthpiece. "He's really worried about you," she whispered.

Helen nodded to Ali that she understood and raised the phone to her ear. "Honey?"

Ali went to her bedroom at the opposite end of the house to give Helen privacy. She stretched out on the bed and the next thing she knew, she woke up and an hour had passed. She sprang up from bed and went to find Helen. She was reading in the living room with classical music playing softly on the radio.

"Helen, how could you let me sleep so long? I never intended to take a nap at all!" Ali told her. "I just wanted to leave you alone while you talked to Eric."

"From the times I've heard you up at night, I know you're not getting a lot of sleep lately. You seemed especially tired today and I hated to wake you."

"Yeah, I've been thinking a lot instead of sleeping lately. But naps don't get my work done." She rubbed her hands together. "I want some lemonade. How about you?"

Helen wanted some too, so Ali headed for the kitchen to fill two glasses. "How's Eric?" she called as she poured. "Is everything okay?"

"Actually it's more than okay between us."

"I'm so glad to hear that."

Ali handed Helen her glass and they settled in the comfortable chairs in the living room.

"I didn't know he was going to do it, but Eric has asked for an assignment that will keep him in one location with little or no travel."

"That's wonderful."

Helen grinned. "He asked for the change so we could be together more. It turned out his boss had the same idea, but for different reasons. Isn't that great? Now he won't be transferred so often."

Ali leaned across the chair to pat her sister's arm. "You'd better believe it's great, Helen. It's fantastic."

"Um, Eric wants to be with me more . . . well, so we can start a family." A wonderful smile filled Helen's face. "And we both want him to be an active part of our family, not merely a visitor to it when he happens to be in town. I wouldn't want to raise children alone if I didn't have to."

Clapping her hands together, Ali hooted. "I am so happy for you," she said deliberately. "This is turning out perfectly for you guys. Do you know when he'll get the transfer?"

"Actually, we'll be moving right away. His boss wants to use Eric's expertise to turn around the Texas operation that's been damaged by the hurricanes down there lately."

Ali frowned with concern for her sister.

"But we'll be living far inland where it's safe. Can you picture me a Texan? Eric said we'll be able to get a house with a yard and lots of space for kids to play."

Ali relaxed again. "But I thought you didn't want to move again?"

"No, but this move is okay. I know Eric is very good at what he does, Ali. I can't deny him that. He's worked and studied hard to get where he is today. The company has to send him where they can put his ability to the best use. But now that he's promoted into management, being in charge of the Texas operation and all, well, the moves won't be nearly as often." She smiled and added, "And I love that he requested the change because he wanted it as much as I did."

Ali looked at her sister's serene, smiling face. "That's what love can do," she said lightly, but all the while, she wondered if that special look would ever be on her face someday when she thought of her Mr. Right.

Jase couldn't believe all the red tape involved and the time it took to get his bakery reopened after the fire. It felt like more than opening the new one. His patience stretched thinner and thinner. At least the oven company had come through quickly to get the new rotating oven installed.

All his other help was local. With the wonderful small town–style helpfulness that was the norm for his company, everyone who worked at the shop as a baker or sales clerk pitched in to help where they were needed most. They put in long hours polishing racks, trays, and showcases after the cleaning service left them water-spotted.

Jase had the staff painting too, when he learned it would be at least two more weeks before professional painters would be available. It wouldn't take professionals to paint everything white again, he reasoned. And the employees who made and sold the baked goods said they would rather help him paint than not work until he opened again.

Though he hadn't been looking for perfection, Jase judged that they did a terrific job. By the time they were finished, only one of the teenaged clerks ended up with what looked like as much paint on him as he'd put on the walls. The kid hadn't needed to admit this was the first time he'd ever painted anything.

While the employees had pulled together and worked during daylight hours, Jase had stayed at the shop to work late every night. His motivation was more than just wanting to put his staff back to work at their regular jobs, or insuring his own business success. A year ago, even six months ago, that would have been enough. Not now. Not since Ali came into his life.

He still hadn't had another chance to talk to her, to come to a mutual understanding of the full situation. Now he couldn't fathom why he'd ever thought deceiving her had been a good idea. He was on the brink of losing the best thing he'd ever had.

"Jase! Jase, the inspector is here," Hank, one of his clerks, called out.

"It's about time," Jase mumbled to himself. The same phrase had popped into his head when he was on the phone, waiting for the inspector's secretary to set up the appointment. But Jase swallowed his complaints. He was painfully aware that the whole business rested on the required permits that gave him the legal right to produce and sell food to the public.

"Mr. Mortimer," Jase read from the nametag hooked on the man's breast pocket. "I'm glad you were able to make it today." He'd almost added "finally" but didn't. "All the folks working for me are counting on us opening again tomorrow so they can get back to drawing a regular paycheck doing what they do best." Though he'd said it with a smile, Jase hoped he hadn't gone too far appealing to Mortimer's humanitarian interests.

"Well now, we'll just see what you've done here first, won't we?"

The fake smile on the man's face would have shown more emotion if it had been cut out of red construction paper and glued on his lips.

Jase forced his own facial expression to stay neutral as he followed Mortimer around the bakery.

Chapter Twelve

At the Liverpool Dutch Treats, the tile floor shone. All the appliances had been polished until they practically glowed. The glass in the showcases sparkled and the countertops were so clean that they looked new.

If the staff could have put things back into place with their fingers crossed, they would have. The last weeks had been a lot of hard work, but Jase had been generous with the bonuses in their paychecks.

Now Jase could tell the employees were wary of the inspector. They knew as well as he did that many small businesses failed despite all the long hours of hard work that went into them. These good people, who had families to support with their work here, all depended on this bakery for their living and needed it to pass the inspection.

As the inspector checked out each area of the operation, Jase walked with him and did his best to defer his own arguments when the man disagreed with him on how something had been done. Mortimer seemed to arbitrarily pick out problem areas.

During the inspection, the deliverymen were carrying in sacks of flour and one hard look by the inspector sent the young workers scurrying for the floor mops to remove his dusty footprints practically before the men toting the sacks had stepped away.

One zealous young helper carrying three giant cans of cherry pie filling had picked up more than he could manage. Twisting his body to lift the heavy tins up to a high shelf, he lost his grip on one of them. He jumped back in time to save his foot from being smashed by the falling missile.

Instead, the can landed on the tiled floor. The bottom of the can caved in and the sides burst outward. The kid's cheeks were as red as the cherry sauce that now decorated a wide area in the storage room.

The *clunk* when the can fell and the kid's yelp alerted the other workers to what had happened. They grabbed the sponges and mops and went after the red goop running across the white walls and floor. By the time the inspector arrived at the storage room door, all he could see were glistening clean tiles.

Jase saw the accident-prone youth standing nearby, his back turned toward Mortimer until the man moved on past him. All his fingers were crossed.

When Mortimer was finally finished, Jase took the report from him. There were only two negative comments listed. Jase heaved a sigh of relief. They were only small cleaning jobs to be completed after the rest of the deliveries were made.

Mortimer could give them the all-clear, though Jase could see he was clearly reluctant to do so without the return visit he'd apparently expected to be necessary. Jase looked at him and waited for his verdict.

"You've done an unbelievably fast cleanup here, VanDam," Mortimer said when he was finished. "That must be some crew you've got working for you. You've passed the inspection."

The cheers from the men and women who stood around waiting to hear the announcement were thrilling. The little smile that appeared on Mortimer's face almost looked sincere. "You'll get the signed certificate in the mail."

Jase shook Mortimer's hand vigorously and thanked him as he walked him to the door. The second he was out of there, Jase headed straight to the phone, where he punched in a number he knew by heart. "Oh, Helen, it's you. I called to tell you both that the bakery just passed inspection. We're about to turn on the ovens so we can bake all afternoon and night and reopen tomorrow."

"Oh, Jase, that's wonderful."

"Thanks, Helen. Ah, is Ali there? Would she talk to me a minute?"

"No, Jase."

"No, she won't?"

"I mean, no, she's not here. She's working on a promotion at a convenience store somewhere right now, but I'll pass on the good word."

"Thanks. And I want to thank you again for your help."

"Oh, that's what neighbors are for," she replied with a weak laugh. "And it gave me a break. I've been so worried about my husband. For nearly a month he's been in the Middle East, where they're working on putting out oil-well fires. It's the most dangerous work he does, and I'm always a nervous wreck until I see him again. In fact, that's why I've been staying with Ali so long. I didn't want to be home alone waiting for him this time."

"I'll bet she's loved having you."

"Well, I've tried to help too. And I think I have. She would have gone bananas putting straws and tops on bottles plus tying on the marketing info if we hadn't done them together."

Jase laughed. "I think you're right. I hope your husband comes home soon—before you know it, Helen."

"Actually, Eric is back in the States now. In fact, he's coming to Syracuse to get me tomorrow. We're going on a little vacation on our way back home. We'll be leaving the day after tomorrow."

"That sounds great. Eric McBride is a lucky man, Helen."

"My husband? Lucky? He knows his job and is good at what he does."

"Yes, I'm sure, but I meant lucky having you for a wife. I know it must mean a lot to him to have you waiting just for him."

"Thanks," she said with a brief laugh. "You're telling me what I do is great, but so many women tell me I'm nuts to stay home and not get a full-time job. I just don't know anymore."

"You have to do what's best for you, and it shouldn't matter what other women think. I can see in the way you talk about Eric that you love him."

"You got that right," she responded. He could hear her smile in her voice.

Jase felt envious. He wanted thoughts of him to please a woman the way Helen had just brightened from thinking about Eric. His mind treated him to an image of Ali. *If only*, he thought.

"Jase?"

"Yeah, I'm here."

"Ali may shoot me, but do you think you would have the time to come over here for dinner tomorrow night to meet Eric?"

"Sure. I'd love to," he told her, glad for the chance to be with Ali again. "I wish your inviting me over meant Ali wasn't still angry with me."

"I can't say that, but you two always seem so happy when you're together."

"Yes. I think she's very special. Helen, I made a big mistake not being completely honest with your sister. I may not deserve another chance, but I'm going to try for one. She means a lot to me."

"I'm glad to hear that, because I think she cares for you even more than she's willing to admit to me. Well, see you tomorrow evening. Six-thirty would be good. Ah, Jase, I think I'm going to forget to tell Ali you're coming."

Jase chuckled. "Thanks, Helen. But if it comes down to telling a lie, don't do it. I don't want to have anything to do with a lie again—not even just a little lie."

"Deal. See you tomorrow."

Jase next turned his mind to the long list of details that had to be taken care of before the first pound of flour could be measured. His crew was carrying in the rest of the heavy sacks and cans like a column of ants. He hurried to the truck to carry in his share. He stepped lightly, knowing he would be spending the next evening with Ali.

The truck was long gone and Jase was putting the recipes in order when one of the assistants who'd been lining the large trays with parchment paper called out, "Will ya get a load of the white stick of dynamite that just pulled into the parking lot. Wow! What do you suppose it is?"

When Jase joined the others at the windows, he let out a whoop. "That is a low, long, white 1957 Thunderbird convertible with red leather interior. And today is my lucky day!"

The driver climbed out and Jase jogged out to meet him. "It looks great!" Jase slapped him on the back and walked all the way around the car. He slid into the driver's seat and turned the key in the ignition. The engine started at once.

"That's the smooth low growl that only a vintage V8 can make." Jase cut the engine and climbed out. "Sounds and looks like you really did it. I can't believe it was possible after the shape the car was in when I found it."

"What do you mean 'found it'?" one of his staff standing behind them asked. "Where can I 'find' one like this for myself?"

"He means it. He did find it," the man who had driven it in said with a laugh. Everyone looked at him expectantly.

"The new bakery we're building—I found it there," Jase explained. "I bought the lot after a fire destroyed the building on it. The guy wanted out and didn't even want to bother to take what was in the garage that was still standing at the back of the driveway. He said I'd have to get rid of the junk in there myself at the low price he was charging for the property."

Shrugging his shoulders, Jase told them, "I said okay. We started to drag out tires and stacks of newspapers from a huge pile. Suddenly the huge pile wasn't all junk, but this car that the junk had been sitting on."

The staff murmured their disbelief and amazement.

"That's when he called me in," the man who had

driven the car into the lot said. "And believe me, it was a mess. Rust. The engine frozen. Hoses all brittle. The tires were flat and the dead weight for decades had damaged the rims. And the inside. You don't want to know what that looked like after generations of mice had made it their home." Everyone agreed with that.

Jase reached out to shake the man's hand. "Thanks. You sure did a great job." His staff applauded.

"Aren't you going to say you're sorry for the hard time you gave me about taking so long to rebuild the thing?"

"No!" Jase responded with a grin. "I've been without a car for far too long. You knew my other car had been totaled by the jerk who stole it, and if you hadn't kept telling me this one would be ready any day now, I would have rented a car weeks ago!"

"Hey, that's right. Now we don't have to drive him to and from work anymore," one of his staff called out. With teasing humor, they cheered the realization.

A brightly painted, original-design Volkswagen Beetle pulled into the lot and came to a stop behind the Thunderbird. Every square inch of the second car's surface, other than the windows, was filled with colorful paintings of dozens of kinds of insects. A Beetle covered with bugs!

Jase laughed and waved to the driver as the man who'd delivered the car jogged over to get in the passenger seat. "Paint that thing over, will you? You're a hazard on the road!"

"You'll be sorry you insulted my artwork," he called over his shoulder with a laugh. "Wait till you get my bill for painting yours!" The Beetle drove off.

"Can I take it for a little spin?" one hopeful youth asked as he passed Jase on his way into the building.

Jase took one more look at the car and dropped the keys into his pocket. "Not on your life!"

They all laughed and turned back to the task of re-stocking the bakery. Soon the air was fragrant with bread rising, vanilla batter mixing with cinnamon and sugar and chocolate. Not even the memory of the smoke smell remained.

Jase doubled his crew that night to make faster head-way in filling the empty racks, even staying on to work himself. They broke in the new oven by running it con-stantly all night long.

"Jase. What are you still doing here?" a voice called to him as morning approached.

"Emma! I might ask the same of you." Jase watched the kindly gray-haired woman who worked for him on weekends walk past him with a pat on his arm. She put her things in her locker before she tied on an apron and scrubbed her hands.

"Jase, you didn't really think I'd let you have all the fun of gearing up to open, did you?" she asked with a grin. "I've got two hours before I have to leave to get to my day job and I want to help."

The others who had worked all night welcomed her. Jase looked at his watch and glanced out at the parking lot to see that he could just begin to distinguish shapes beyond the overhead lights. Dawn. "Where has the night gone?" He stretched. "My shoulders are so spent from work they're numb," Jase said to no one in particular.

"Go home to bed. We can get along without you for a few hours," Emma told him with a grin.

"I think I will," he replied with a tired smile.

Jase tugged at the ties on his apron and saw that his fingers trembled. He tried to ignore it as he had the other times he'd put in such a long stretch of intensive work. "Thanks, Emma."

"Sweet dreams," she responded with a wave of the whisk in her hand. She smiled and got right back to work.

Jase felt worse than exhausted, but he could finally go home. He checked with the others to satisfy himself everything was going as planned and then left.

The night air felt cool against his overheated skin. He inhaled deeply. Probably more rain on the way. He thought about the dousing Ali had given him in the parking lot that day after a heavy rain. It seemed so long ago. He wouldn't have missed it for anything, because it let him get to know her.

Jase climbed into his sleek car and drove across town toward home. He wished he had just the short trip from the bakery near there and not all the way from Liverpool. But at this hour few other cars were on the streets. He took the highway bypass, and when he exited closer to his destination, he began to hit red lights.

At the first one he drummed his thumbs on the steering wheel, impatiently waiting for the green. "Come on, light. Change!"

His shoulders ached and his legs felt so sluggish that it was work to raise his foot to the brake pedal and clutch at the next red light. Almost home. He shifted into neutral and looked left and right. No cars coming. This was a waste of his time to sit there for nothing.

Headlights coming up behind him reflected off the rearview mirror, making his tired eyes hurt and eliminating his bad idea to go through the red light. Jase leaned back against the headrest and closed his eyes to avoid the glare. He rubbed the reddened lids with his knuckles and then blinked rapidly, but his eyes didn't want to stay open. He could just rest his eyes until the light changed, and then open them again to drive on, he thought. How wonderful it would be to stretch out in his bed to sleep.

Moments later, Jase's hands slid down past the leather wheel cover onto his thighs. When the light turned green, his eyes were still closed and his breathing steady in sleep.

Chapter Thirteen

Ali had a terrible time falling asleep. She'd found a tiny bag of chocolate candy with raspberry centers from A Real Sweetie tied to her doorknob early the day before. Jase's phone number was on the bag. As if she could have forgotten it.

Or forgotten him.

Now she was lying in bed awake. Again. Every night since the scene in his office when she had confronted him about his deception, Ali had lain awake thinking of what Jase had done. The lie had only been to hide that he had money. He hadn't lied the way Jeff did, for personal gain. Her eyes popped open. He certainly hadn't been out to steal her money, as Jeff had done. He was definitely not a crook.

In comparing the two men, was she also confusing

them? And confusing her feelings for them? Had Jase been right when he said she was making more out of his lie because of what Jeff had done?

I was so angry at Jeff, she thought. *I trusted him and he led me on. He said he loved me and yet he stole all the money I'd been saving for our house.*

She rolled over and punched at her pillow. She had thought she loved him, but now when she thought about it, she didn't think it had been love. She'd certainly never felt toward Jeff what she felt for Jase. Jeff paid attention to her, said the right things to her, but he'd never meant a word. Everything he said was a lie. He kept talking about their future together, and he must have known all along there would be no future for them at all.

With a start she realized she was still giving Jeff the power to hurt her after all this time. Turning her back on Jase hurt them both deeply. "No more. My past with Jeff is over and done," she said aloud. Freed from her past, she could only hope that she still had a future with Jase.

Ali slipped into a fitful sleep. Only a few hours later, she stirred, but she wasn't sure what woke her. The light of dawn glowed in the sky, but the light couldn't have been bright enough to wake her. She listened to the silence and couldn't make out any unusual sound.

Throwing back the sheet, she crossed to the window to look out beside the drape. Two cars were coming down the street. The first one was an incredible vintage convertible, though it was hard to tell exactly what kind in faint light. She wondered who owned a car like that in this neighborhood. Before now, she'd only seen one like it in movies.

Her gaze skipped to the second car, a police patrol car, but its red flashers were not turned on. Both cars slowed as they approached the driveway between her house and Jase's.

Ali dropped the window drape, grabbed her terry robe, and pulled it on as she ran barefoot through the house to open her kitchen door.

She peered out the screen door and saw Jase getting out of the vintage car. She leaned forward to see two police officers emerge from their car a short distance down the driveway. The driver remained by his door and the other officer came to the front of their cruiser.

"Thanks for the escort home, fellas. I'm fine now," Jase told them with a little wave of his arm.

Ali must have made a sound, because the patrolmen looked over to see her behind the screen. Jase glanced over at her and winced when he met her gaze but didn't say anything to her. He looked away and shifted his weight from one foot to the other.

"Appreciate the escort," Jase said, waving his hand to dismiss the officers. "Good night." He looked relieved that they took the hint and climbed into their car.

Silently, he watched them drive down the street and turn the corner out of sight before he grabbed a white Dutch Treats bag from the front seat and closed the car door. Then he walked straight toward Ali's door. One arm braced on the side of her screen door, he lifted his head to study her face but didn't speak.

Ali looked at the car and then back at Jase. "Is that the car that's been in the shop for weeks?"

"Yeah. I had another car, nearly new, in fact. But it was stolen the weekend before I moved in. I was working late at the main office. Some kids took it for a joyride and totaled it. And the kids didn't have a scratch on them. They were too high and relaxed to get hurt."

"Here I thought . . . Well, it doesn't matter what I thought. What happened to require a police escort? Are you all right?" She stopped and held up her hand before he had a chance to answer. "No, no. I'm sorry I asked. It's none of my business."

"Yes it is, Ali. I appreciate your concern for me. But nothing happened. I fell asleep at a stoplight on the way home. Those guys pulled up behind me. Once I convinced them that I wasn't drunk, they followed me home to make sure I got here safely. End of story." He stared at her a moment and heaved a sigh but didn't move.

Ali saw the pained expression on his face. She was surprised he'd wanted to tell her what happened. After all, there was no longer a reason to share his life with her, and doing so must have made him uncomfortable. "What do you want, Jase? Do you want to come in?"

"No, after baking all through the night on top of working all yesterday, too, I don't dare sit down. I'd fall asleep right there in your kitchen. But I brought you these." He held up the bag. "I wanted you to have some of our first Danish and croissants for your breakfast with Helen—a token to thank you both for your help the day after the fire at the store."

She opened the door and took the bag from him. "Thank you." She held the door open with her foot and clutched the bag with both hands.

"We open tomorrow. I mean today." He looked at his watch and shook his head. "In less than an hour, actually." He looked back at her. "We reopened as fast as we could. So the new store opening will stand on its own. But Wilson's already told you that you can go ahead with the promotion plans for the grand opening."

Ali lowered her gaze to the bag and leaned over to set it on the end of the counter. "No, I'm not doing the promotion for Dutch Treats, Jase. I resigned right after you left the meeting in your office. I sent Frank a letter putting my resignation in writing the next day. He's probably found someone else by now. You don't need me." She stepped back to allow the door to close.

Pushing the door open, Jase lunged for her arm and caught her wrist before she was out of reach. The screen bounced against his elbow. "There's where you're all wrong, Ali." He stepped up from the stoop through the door. Their gazes locked. "I do need you. And I need to talk to you to make you understand just how much. Without knowing you or giving you a chance to be different, I boxed you up in the same package with other women who have shown interest in me only because of my money. Once I'd gotten to know you, I knew I was wrong. Very wrong."

He looked intently at her face as if studying her before he spoke again. "Alison deGroot, let's get one thing straight right now. I told you I'm sorry I was less than completely honest with you. I've never regretted anything as much in my whole life. If I'd known how I was going to feel about you, I would have told you, or at least not tried to hide the fact that I owned Dutch Treats. But I kept it from you. And I hurt you. I'm sorry, but it's over and done—just like your problems with Jeff should be. And I promise you I will never deceive you again."

"You . . ."

Jase put his fingers gently on her lips to silence them. "The thing is that starting right now, I'm going to right my wrong to you, Ali. I'm going to prove to you that I trust you to know everything there is to know about me. I'm going to deserve your trust in me."

Tears stung her eyes and made her blink rapidly. "I never gave you a reason to lie to me," she said in a voice hoarse with emotion.

"I know. I know. And I never set out to lie to you. You may find this hard to believe, but when the women I used to date found out that I own Dutch Treats, I knew their attraction was to my money, not to me. But when I met you," he added with a smile, "I discovered I needed any attraction you felt to be only to me, not my money, only me."

"You think that I . . ."

"No, Ali, I don't. That's the whole point. That's exactly why I tried to hide the fact that I own the bakeries. I know that however you feel about me, even if you hate me now, it's a feeling you have for me and not for my owning a chain of stores. You see, I needed to know that it was me you seemed to like being with, not my money."

He snorted a little laugh. "I couldn't get over it. You actually wanted to buy your own dinner when we went out for our first dinner together. No woman since my mother years ago has ever offered to pay for her dinner when we were out together. That felt nice. But when I'd figured out I could tell you about myself, I still wasn't in a real hurry to do so. For the first time, I was seeing a woman who liked me. Just me. It was a wonderful feeling. Heady stuff. Just being with you makes me feel good."

A sob escaped Ali and he drew her into his arms, resting his chin on the top of her head. "Oh, Ali. What I'm trying to tell you is that I . . ."

"No. Stop. Not now." Ali's heart pounded in her ears. She felt the weight of his arms as he leaned heavily on her. "Jase, you're too tired to talk more now. You're almost too tired to stand up. Let's see each other and talk more after you've slept."

"You'll see me tomorrow? I mean later today?"

"Yes, I promise. Now go home to bed."

He stepped back and smiled. "Okay, I'll wait and tell

you later. If you'll excuse me then . . . Oh, did I mention that I have a dinner date tonight with the woman next door? I'd better get right to sleep because I don't want to be too tired for it."

Ali scrunched up her brow and tipped her head a little to the side. "You're having dinner with the lady next door?"

"Yeah. Her sister invited me last night when I called to let them know that we'd passed inspection."

"What? Oh, now I understand." She folded her arms over her ribs.

"Her sister didn't tell her, huh?"

Ali smiled and shook her head. "Not a word. The lady probably wouldn't have found out until her sister took out the fourth dinner plate, or until you walked in the door."

"I hope the lady doesn't mind that I'm coming."

Ali looked at him a moment and then unfolded her arms and let them fall to her sides. "Actually, she's very pleased that you're coming."

"Good. I hear I'm going to get to meet more of my neighbor's family, and I want to impress them."

"I think you'll do just fine. Her family likes you already."

"Good." He leaned down to kiss her gently, only to interrupt the kiss and lift his face for a big yawn.

Ali chuckled. "It doesn't do a lot for the woman being kissed to have the man suddenly yawn right in the middle."

"I'll more than make it up to you on the next one. I promise," Jase said with a chuckle.

"Go home," she urged. With her hands on his shoulders, she turned him toward his house. "I'll see you at dinner." She gave him a little shove and watched until he disappeared into his house.

The sun had risen and illuminated a clear blue sky. It wasn't long before the scent of the coffee Ali made brought Helen into the kitchen. "Good morning," Helen said brightly. "Is that decaf?"

"No, but I can make some quick in the little pot."

"Yeah, thanks. I'm going to lay off caffeine and see if I can still stay awake during the day," Helen replied with a grin.

"Nice to see you with a smile on your face."

"Not an easy feat at this early hour, but I might say the same about you."

"Yeah, I guess I am smiling. Jase just came home. I went to the door when I heard him drive up. He was so tired I hope he didn't fall asleep before he got into bed."

Ali looked at her sister to discover her yawning. "Then there's you, Helen. Jase stays awake more and more while you sleep more and more—every chance you get, in fact. Hardly an afternoon goes by that you don't take a nap and you're yawning already this morning."

Ali took a bite out of a heavenly croissant that she'd lifted from the Dutch Treats bag. She looked back at Helen and tossed her the bag. "There's one for you too, from Jase."

"Well, he can't help but be tired with his work and crazy hours." She broke off a piece and chewed it, her grin growing. "But I've got just as good an excuse, Ali."

"What do you mean, you have an excuse? You're not just a vacationer being lazy?" Ali looked over from making the second pot of coffee to see the calmest smile come across her sister's face.

"That too, but I'm pregnant."

"Oh, Helen!" Ali stepped over to give her a big hug. "I'm so happy for you. Why didn't you say something before? Oh, dear. You are happy about it, aren't you? You always said you wanted to have children."

"Yes, Eric and I are both very happy. And I'm sorry I haven't told you before, but I needed to let the idea sink in, and I . . . Well, I was bursting to tell you, but I wanted to tell Eric first. Then there was the fire at Jase's bakery, and you've been so upset . . ."

"I can understand that and I don't mind. Really. Oh, Helen. All the work you did at the bakery. Are you all right?"

"I don't call that very hard work and yes, I'm fine, silly. I'm pregnant, not ill. But I think that's why I got a little queasy that day when I saw the dumped food. I've only felt a little morning sickness so far and I've got my fingers crossed that I don't feel any more."

Ali grinned as she sat at the table opposite her sister. "I'm going to be an aunt. Auntie Ali. Is that nice, or what?"

Helen took Ali's hand in hers. "You're going to make

a great aunt, Ali. Jase wouldn't be any slouch as an uncle either."

"Better not let Eric hear you talking about the neighborhood hunk like that. Hey. How would you like some scrambled eggs with the croissant?"

"Perfect. You know, I could get used to getting waited on like this, lying in the shade of a maple tree all day, reading good books. I wonder if Eric would go for waiting on me? Maybe I'll ask him when we pick him up at the airport this morning."

The sisters laughed as Ali broke the eggs into a bowl for their breakfast.

Chapter Fourteen

With a loaf of French bread tucked under his arm, Jase wore a smile as he exited his kitchen door that evening. Freshly showered and a whole lot more rested after a good day's sleep, he was eager to see Ali. Laughter and music floated his way from her backyard. The party atmosphere seemed very appropriate for all he had to celebrate now.

As he crossed to her side of the driveway and approached her backyard gate, he could see the three of them on the raised deck behind her house. The tall man with reddish-blond hair had to be Eric. He had an open and honest face. Jase knew he would like getting to know him. Helen was reclining in grand style in Ali's comfortable-looking wide chaise, punctuating something she said with the bottle of water in her hand.

Between them, Ali stood at the table biting into a piece of carrot she'd just coated with a green dip. The sight of her filled him with happiness.

"Did you save some of that for me?" Jase asked Ali in a voice made husky by the effect she had on him.

Ali turned toward him, and her face brightened into a warm, welcoming smile. Jase released the breath he'd been holding as she closed the distance to meet him at the deck steps.

She held her hand out to him. Jase leapt up the two steps, letting her know how eager he was. Taking her hand in his, he kissed her smiling upturned lips. He couldn't help himself, and when he lifted his face to look into hers, he was glad he had. Instead of shrinking away, she was smiling and still holding his hand. The way she looked at him lifted a heavy weight off his heart, and he couldn't help but smile broadly himself.

"It's been a struggle, but I managed to save you some of each of the veggies that go with the dip." Ali turned to glare at Eric with an exaggerated scowl. "Even though a certain someone here has been gobbling it all up like it was about to become extinct from the face of the earth."

"Hey, what can I say? I've been on the road a month without any home cooking. Even Ali's tastes good," Eric exclaimed to Jase with a shrug.

Helen elbowed her husband for his good-natured teasing.

Ali pulled Jase across the deck to the others. "Jase,

this spinach-dip hound is Eric McBride, Helen's husband, aaannnd . . . I have just learned today, the proud father of her fetus."

"I beg your pardon?" Jase looked down at Helen and then back at Eric. He extended a hand, which Eric shook heartily.

"What the funny lady means is that we're going to be a daddy." The trio laughed. "I mean I'll be the daddy and Helen will be the mommy."

"That's better," Helen noted.

His hand freed, Eric placed it back on Helen's shoulder with a loving squeeze. Her hand immediately covered his.

"Congratulations. And to you too, Helen. That's great." Jase leaned down and kissed Helen's cheek easily, as if they'd been friends for years. She smiled up at him.

"Now we have two things to celebrate here tonight," Eric offered.

Jase looked back at Ali. She shrugged. "Two things?" he asked Eric.

"Yeah, your store reopened today, didn't it? The women have been telling me about your fire and the mess you had to clean up," Eric commiserated. "That was a tough break."

Jase nodded. "It could have been a lot worse. If the fire had gotten out of hand, the blaze could have been horrendous with all the flour and sugar stored there. It could have been explosive, in fact."

"I was surprised to hear how fast you turned it all back to normal and opened up for business again. I wish I could turn around some of the botched-up oil rigs they give me to fix that fast."

"It was only possible thanks to a lot of great people working very hard. I'm very glad it's all behind us now."

"And you know for sure the sprinkler system works," Helen said, making them all laugh.

Ali tugged at Jase's arm. "Come in the kitchen, Jase. You can open the bottle of sparkling grape juice I bought while I get the glasses."

In the kitchen, while Ali reached to the top shelf for tall slender glasses, Jase set down the bread and got the juice bottle from the refrigerator. When she lowered the glasses to the counter, he placed his hands on her shoulders to tug her into his arms. "I've missed being with you so much since the fire."

She remained too stiff for his liking, so he relaxed his hold and looked down at her face. He'd have to settle for the small smile, though he would have liked to see one that made her eyes sparkle.

"We still have a lot to talk over, Jase. And, um . . . Your marketing manager called again today about the contract. It seems he doesn't want to take my 'no thanks' for an answer."

He inhaled deeply and shook his head. "Ali, I'm not sure what the contract means to you, but having the promotion done well by the most capable person means a lot to me. I was being completely honest when I said I had nothing to do with awarding the contract. When I learned a little about your business through the problems with the candy bags, I didn't even know exactly what you did. Later, when I learned more about it and realized you might apply for the job, I took myself out of the position of being judge."

"Don't remind me. All you knew was that I'd made a mistake in one of my promotions and let your phone number go out on the candy bags," she said ruefully. "All you knew then was how bad I was." She groaned.

Jase smiled. "I knew that was the printer's error. It wasn't your fault. And I also knew you handled it and made it right. I admired that, but I never told Wilson anything—either about my number on the bags or how you handled correcting the problem. He decided you were the best person for the job without any input from me. That's the way I wanted it, and I knew that's the way you would want it too."

She nodded.

"But I was tempted to tell him how great you were. I wanted him to know you are bright and very capable, creative and very hard-working."

"If I ever need a one-man cheering section, I'll know who to turn to," Ali responded with a grin.

He raised his hand to cradle her jaw. "Ali, I didn't tell you early this morning, but I've got to tell you now. I'm in love with you. I love you. However you want me to say it so you'll believe me, I will. I don't know what the future holds for us, but I do know I care about you in a way I've never cared for any other woman. I love being with you. And I'm not keeping any more secrets from you."

"No more deceptions?" she whispered as one little tear of joy moistened her eyes.

Jase shook his head. "None. Not even sweet, chocolate-frosted deceptions."

He rubbed his thumb gently across her cheek. Ali turned her head and kissed his hand as he caressed her cheek.

"Jase, I'm sorry I mixed up my feelings of anger and resentment for Jeff with what I feel for you. Whatever happens between us, I have to be able to trust you completely—with my heart and with my life." She smiled. "But now I know I can, and I already love you."

Jase hugged her and cradled her head against his shoulder. "I don't know how I managed to earn your love in return, but thank you." He kissed her sweet-smelling hair and leaned back so he could see her face. "And I'm going to make sure you never change your mind."

Ali slid her arms around his neck. "Jase, I don't want anything to come between us again."

"I'm counting on that, because I intend to court you."

"Court me?" Ali croaked. "I haven't heard that word in years."

"Yeah. Does it sound too old-fashioned for you?"

"No. It sounds wonderful," she whispered.

"Ali, I'm going to ask you to marry me just as soon

as I'm certain you'll say yes. I couldn't stand it if you said no."

Ali rose up on her toes and kissed him softly. "Then you had better eat a lot for dinner. You'll need your strength for the shock when I say yes."

Jase lowered his head, very intent on kissing her again, when Eric slid open the deck screen door and entered the kitchen.

"Oops! Helen told me not to come in here now. I asked her what could be taking so long just getting glasses and she laughed. I should have listened to her. She said you two could take care of everything. Looks like you're doing fine too. Ah . . . Both of you."

Laughing, Ali turned in Jase's arms. He reluctantly let her move away so she could put the glasses on a small tray that she pulled out from the cabinet.

"Now see what you've done," Jase complained with mock anger.

"Hey, I didn't mean to interrupt," Eric said with a laugh and a shrug. "I just came in because I wanted to tell you the charcoal is ready."

"Good," Ali said, her back still to him. "You take these glasses, Eric. I'll bring the steak kabobs from the fridge. Jase, can you open the sparkling grape juice on the deck?"

"Sure thing."

Instead of moving to pick up the glasses, Eric stepped to his sister-in-law's side and put his hand on her arm. Looking right into her eyes, he asked, "Everything's okay? This guy's intentions are honorable, aren't they?" He motioned toward Jase with a nod of his head and a jerk of his thumb, gangster-movie style. "I don't have to take him out in the backyard and show him a thing or two, do I now?"

Ali put her arms around Eric and hugged him. "Thanks, brother dear, but no way! If anyone goes out with Jase in the backyard or anywhere else, it's going to be me."

"Whew! That's a relief, Ali. Have you noticed his biceps?" Jase joked. "And I'd much rather go out with you. You're a whole lot cuter than he is." Laughing, Eric feigned a punch to Jase's shoulder. "But you needn't worry, Eric. I'll have you know that my intentions are very honorable."

"I'm counting on that," Eric said in a response that sounded very much like a warning, no matter how nicely delivered.

Jase smiled and grabbed a dishtowel. He folded it over his arm like a wine steward. Making a big show of it, he straightened his shirt lapels and smoothed his hair before he picked up the bottle of grape juice.

"Terribly good show, old boy," Ali teased.

Eric carried the glasses out to the deck with Jase right behind him.

Ali lifted the meat tray from the refrigerator and closed the door with her hip. She looked out at the three people she loved most in the world. A broad smile on her face, she joined the others on the deck.

After a theatrical bow, Jase opened the bottle of bubbly juice. Helen held the glasses for him once the cork popped out. Ali laid the speared pieces of meat and vegetables on the rack over the glowing coals while Jase handed out the filled glasses. The smiles never left their faces.

Jase handed her a glass when she stepped back to his side. He raised his glass to make a toast. "Here's to Eric's safe arrival back in the States and to the wonderful surprise he and Helen have shared with us about the baby."

"Hear, hear!" the others cheered and drank a sip.

Eric contributed a toast. "And here's to the reopened bakery."

"Thank you," Jase responded. "You women have my deep appreciation for your neighborly help over there and for your moral support despite other . . . difficulties."

A special look of love passed between Jase and Ali. "To the bakeries," she toasted and they all drank another sip.

"Aaannnd . . ." Jase's extended word made Eric and Helen pause with their glasses in the air and look back at him. His broad smile was a twin to the one Ali wore as he circled his arm around her waist and pulled her to his side.

"And here's to Ali, who has forgiven a big mistake I made," he said. Their gazes were locked and each smiled. "I've forewarned her that I intend to convince her to marry me. I only hope I can bring her as much happiness as she brings me."

Eric congratulated the happy couple as they all drank to their happiness. "Helen, I always did like your sister," Eric added. "And I think I'm going to like Jase too."

"I know I do already," Helen said. "Anyone who can create delicious confections the way he does has got to be sweet through and through."

Jase laughed. "I'd take a bow, but I can't until after we eat. I might topple over from hunger. I was so beat this morning when I finally got home that I fell asleep without eating first, and I'm starved."

Everyone laughed and pitched in to get dinner barbequed and served. The first thing Ali did was pick up a piece of broccoli and cover the rounded end of it with some of her spinach dip. Her other hand flattened under it to catch any drips, she stepped over to Jase with a smile on her face.

"Here, you sweet man. We don't want you to pass out from hunger before the meat's done cooking." She popped the vegetable into his open mouth.

"Hey, this is good."

That bite and several more he snitched on each trip to the deck tided him over until their dinner was ready.

Helen settled herself back into the chaise, her plate of food on her lap, and held out her hand to Eric, who came to sit on the edge of the cushion by her knees, his plate balanced on his thighs.

Ali sat in one of the padded straight-backed chairs while Jase leaned against the railing beside her. When he wasn't eating, he rested his hand on her shoulder. His warm thumb turned lazy little circles on her upper arm.

She understood his need to touch. The man she'd thought was a Mr. Not Right was actually a perfect Mr. Right. And now she needed the contact with him too, to confirm the precious loving tie that existed between them—unfettered by deception.